Two for the River

MR. L. P. HARTLEY'S new collection of stories, *Two for the River*, shows the same qualities of imagination, humour and interest in the macabre which were displayed in *The White Wand* and his earlier tales.

The title story deals with a malevolent swan which unwittingly saves the writer's house for him; seldom can the royal birds have been more closely observed or more bitterly resented. 'Per Far L'Amore' is set in the Venice that Mr. Hartley knows so well, and describes a father's search for his missing daughter, with a climax reminiscent of a famous scene in *The Go-Between*. 'A Very Present Help' is one of two stories in which housekeepers play important roles, and Mr. Hartley has written few better character-studies than his portrayal of the diffident George Lambert tortured by his young mistress and saved by his housekeeper.

Amongst the macabre stories, 'Someone in the Lift', 'The Corner Cupboard', 'The Pampas Clump' and 'The Waits' stand out. And his humour is at its best in 'Cross Purposes', 'A High Dive' and 'Won by a Fall'.

We are proud to publish these stories by the author of whom Miss Storm Jameson wrote recently in *The Sunday Times*: 'He is the most urbane, the most delicately penetrating of novelists.'

Two for the River

BY

L. P. HARTLEY

HAMISH HAMILTON

LONDON

First published in Great Britain, 1961
by Hamish Hamilton Ltd
90 Great Russell St London WC1
Copyright © 1961 by L. P. Hartley

338337

PRINTED IN GREAT BRITAIN BY
WESTERN PRINTING SERVICES LTD BRISTOL

407904-3

Contents

Two for the River

MID-AUGUST was a dull time in my garden—the drought had seen to that. Flowers there were, but even the hardiest were only half their normal size; the Japanese anemones looked like shillings, not half-crowns. Because the garden lay beside the river, and sometimes, in wet seasons, under it, people thought the subsoil must be moist, but it was not; the rain ran off the steep slope without sinking in, the river drained the ground without irrigating it.

But the river-banks had just been in full glory, two interminable winding borders on which grew willow-weed and loosestrife, the lilac clusters of hemp agrimony, deep yellow ragwort, lemon-yellow chickweed, the peeping purple of the woody nightshade, the orange drops of the ranunculus, the youthful, tender teazle-cones of palest pink contrasting with their hard, brown, dried-up predecessors of the year before—and, a newcomer to the district but very much at home, the tall white balsam. Did the other flowers realize their danger from this rampant stranger with its innocent baby-face? Did they foresee the day when it, and only it, would occupy their standing room, making a close-set jungle through which a man could hardly force his way—while the plants, if it was their shooting season, popped off their pods at him? Nor would the invasion stop at the river-bank; it would follow up its conquest through the meadows. And how would the fishermen fare, who even now had to hack out from the massed vegetation

A*

steps and nests for themselves on competition days? Only the
water-lilies would be safe, and the armies of reeds and rushes—
the sword-shaped ones of yellow-green, the round pike-shafts
of bluish-green, tufted with pennons—for they would have the
water to protect them.

On garden and river-bank alike autumn had already laid its
spoiling finger, bringing languor and disarray to the luxuriance
of summer, making it flop and sprawl. To this the river itself
bore witness, for on its grey-green surface floated the earliest
victims of the year's decline, yellow willow leaves tip-tilted like
gondolas, that twirled and sported in the breeze, until the
greedy water sucked them under.

But the flowers grew farther upstream. On my stretch of the
river there were none; trees overhung it on both sides, on mine
a copper beech, a mountain ash, a square-cut bay-tree, a silver
birch, a box elder, and in the corner by the boathouse,
threatening its foundations, a dome-capped sycamore. A low
stone wall divided the river from the garden, which was
narrow for its length and sloping steeply to the lawn; and
from the outward-curving terrace in front of the house you
could see the river, a mirror broken here and there by tree-
trunks, and darkened by the reflections of the trees on the
farther bank; or maybe by the image of a cow, suspended in
mid-water upside-down, the shadowy feet seeming almost to
touch the real feet. Sometimes these reflections were clearer
than the things reflected, so little current was there in the
summer, or breeze to ruffle them. But faithful likenesses
though they were, they had no colour, except a darker shade of
olive-green. The river imposed its own colour on everything
it looked at, even the sky.

'Shall I bathe?' I thought. Flanking the boathouse was a
flight of steps, ending in a large square flagstone, only a few
inches above the water level. Ideal for a dive! And the water
was deep almost at once, twenty feet deep, some said; I hadn't

plumbed it. It did invite me. I laid aside my pen, for I was writing in the open air, a thing I seldom do—the open air has so many distractions, so many claims on one's attention: the river itself, for instance! But no, it was too late to bathe: the August sun hung over Follet Down, and my circulation wasn't what it used to be. Tomorrow at midday, perhaps...

As I was taking up my pen again, with the dull, cold sense of self-congratulation that an unwilling act of prudence some-times brings, I saw a ripple spreading on the river, convex at first, then slightly concave. It was the swans, angry as usual. What trouble those odious birds had given me! He, the cob, was much the worse of the two; she was a nasty creature, with a supercilious, inquisitive expression, but she only aided and abetted him. He was a demon. An inveterate oarsman with a large experience of swans, I had often thought that this one was possessed: Jupiter in disguise perhaps, or not even in dis-guise. He seemed to think I had designs on her. A Leda-complex! I shouldn't have thought of bathing if I'd known he was about, for he had a bad record with bathers. And with boaters a worse one; but I was his favourite target. He had only to see me in my skiff to go for me. It was a slender craft, hard to trim and easily upset: if I had had hair enough to matter I should have parted it in the middle. His methods of attack varied from in-fighting, when he would try to get his wing under the boat, to dive-bombing tactics. These were still more alarming. Spying me from afar he would come after me, skimming over the water and then, when I was bracing myself to take the impact of this living rocket, subside behind me in a smother of foam. The four-barred iron seat in the stern de-fended me: he dared not risk collision with it. But he had found a way round it, and now his system was to by-pass the stern and try to land on one of the sculls. So far he had missed his mark, but if he hit it...

What was he up to now? With snaky neck pressed down

between outward-curving wings held taut for flight, he was forcing his way upstream with powerful thrusts, using his feet for oars, as the Greek poet said. Behind him at a discreet distance came his mate, paddling feverishly, but with neck erect, not battened down as his was. Had they seen another swan perhaps, an interloper? For this was *their* reach of the river, as it had been mine, before they came, and they would not tolerate another swan on it.

They passed on, out of sight, but his baleful, malignant presence lingered with me; I have never seen, in any creature, such devilish intent as flashed from that wicked eye. Swollen with anger, he looked twice the size of other swans. Had it become a struggle for mastery between us? Did he embody some spirit of opposition to me, that the place had? I loved it, but since I bought it, eleven years ago, so many vexatious and frustrating things had happened. . . .

Now all was peace. The river had regained its glassy surface and restored the sense of quietude which the contemplation of still water nearly always gives me. Just as the sudden cessation of a noise—a dog barking or someone hammering—induces sleep, so did the let-up in my swan-resentment prepare my mind for more congenial guests. Now for some real work.

Or so I promised myself, and rested my elbows on the iron table, painted green to match the garden. But my musings were once more interrupted before they became fertile. Another ripple spread across the river, and before I had time to wonder if it heralded another swan, I heard the sound of voices, a man's voice and a woman's. This didn't surprise me. Boats, other than mine, were infrequent on the river, because of the weir, half a mile below, that protected it from the populous reach used by the townspeople. But hardier spirits sometimes lifted their boats round the weir and went on upstream into the unspoilt countryside.

Instead of carrying on past me, as I thought they would, the voices seemed to become stationary, and changed their tone. From being desultory they became animated; from being animated, argumentative. Which of the two prevailed I still don't know, but it was the man who called out to me.

'Sir!'

I was only a stone's throw from them, and not many feet above them, but as I am a little deaf I got up from my table, rather unwillingly, and went down the steps through the rockery and across the lawn in the direction the sounds came from. Leaning over the wall I saw them, in a smart, light new canoe, the man, who sat behind, holding on to the big flagstone that served as my diving-board.

I suppose they hadn't seen or heard me coming, for they looked up as if I was an apparition. They were both very fair, in their late twenties, I should guess, and both very good-looking—she especially. She had a longish face, deep blue eyes, and corn-gold hair piled high on her head. They were both wearing white.

He was the first to speak.

'Sir,' he said again (perhaps it was a tribute to my age), 'you must excuse us, but we wondered if you would let us use your landing-stage to change places in the boat? You see we are not skilled canoeists, and my wife is rather tired of paddling always on one side. We mustn't change places in mid-stream, I'm told. If you would allow us to land for a moment—'

His pleasant voice, her questioning, self-deprecatory smile, and their unassuming air (boating brings out rowdyism in so many people) made me take to them.

'Of course,' I said. 'But aren't you tired, having come all the way from Warmwell? Why not stop and have a drink, one for the river, before you go on?'

They exchanged a doubtful look. Does the prospect bore them? I thought, instantly suspicious. But the woman said:

'You're very kind. We'd like to.'

'Let me give you a hand,' I said. 'You mustn't rock the boat too much'—a timely warning, as it turned out, for they made a very awkward landing. 'I told you we were amateurs,' the man said. 'In fact we only bought this canoe yesterday. We're on our honeymoon; it's almost the first thing we've bought since we were married! We're staying in Warmwell to house-hunt,' he went on, 'and the river looked so inviting with the swans by Paulet Bridge, and all—we thought it would be fun to have our own boat, and go prospecting. That's what brought us here! But it's an awkward piece of luggage to travel with. Perhaps we shall give it away. But I hope—'

By this time we were half-way across the lawn. They fitted their long strides to mine; their graceful, white-clad figures were so tall I wondered how they tucked themselves into the boat.

We had drinks in my study, a darkish room in spite of its three windows. The creepers I once planted had rampaged. The jessamine looked in at one window, too intrusively, and the other two were darkened by the clematis which dripped from the veranda in untidy loops and streamers. But my visitors were enchanted.

'So this is where you work?' the woman asked.

'Yes, but how did you know?'

She looked towards my disorderly writing-desk, and smiling, shook her head.

'I recognize the signs ... Besides—' she caught her husband's eye and stopped.

While I was pouring out the drinks a sort of telepathic communication stirred in me.

'Did you come out looking for a house?' I ventured.

Again they exchanged glances.

'In a way,' the man said. 'The agent told us—'

'Yes?'

'That there was a house on the river that might be for sale. We wondered if we could spot it.'

'Was that why you stopped and hailed me?'

They both coloured.

'No,' he said. 'We genuinely wanted to change places, for Sylvia was getting tired. My name is Harry,' he said hastily. 'Harry Marchmont. We're not the impostors that perhaps we look! But we did just think—'

'That this house was for sale?'

He nodded.

'Well, I'm the owner of it,' I said, 'and I can assure you that it isn't.'

I spoke more stiffly than I meant to, but one or two other people had been sent by agents to make the same inquiry. Why had it got about that I meant to sell the house? They blushed again, more deeply than before.

'Oh, we are so sorry,' Mrs. Marchmont said, while her husband made inarticulate noises of apology. 'Of course there are several other houses by the river—'

'But not owned by a writer,' said I, giving their embarrassment no time to wear off, 'and not quite on the river. They are cut off from it by a tow-path.'

'I'm sure they're not half so nice as this one,' Mrs. Marchmont said. She drained her glass. 'Now, Harry, we must be getting on our way, and not waste any more of Mr. . . . . Mr. Minchin's time.'

So they knew my name, too.

We were all on our feet, the smiles of goodbye stiffening our faces, when to my great surprise I heard myself saying:

'But as you're here, won't you look over the house?'

In some confusion, protesting that they mustn't, that it was an imposition, that they had already trespassed too much on my kindness, they agreed.

We made a tour of the house, and they professed themselves delighted with everything they saw. At first their comments were strictly those of sightseers. 'Oh, what a lovely view! And that church tower between the trees on the hill! Has anybody painted it?' But soon their reactions grew more personal, and sharpened by the excitement of possible possession. 'This room would be perfect for a nursery, wouldn't it? Just put bars across the windows and a little gate outside to shut off the staircase . . . Are you married, Mr. Minchin?'

I was used to this question from women who were strangers to me.

'No.'

'Do you live in this big house all alone?'

'I'm overhoused, but several people live here; they help me in various ways, and I give them house-room. On the whole they seem contented.'

What uphill work it was, in these days, trying to run a private house! They were anachronisms, really. But the depression I sometimes felt about my domestic situation, which was so much easier than most people's, came of having no one at hand to grumble to, no confidant. Whereas this couple—

Mrs. Marchmont was saying: 'Of course we shouldn't want to alter anything. A bathroom here or there, perhaps . . .'

'My dear, you mustn't talk like that. It's Mr. Minchin's house, and he doesn't want to sell it.'

'Of course not, Mr. Minchin, I was just day-dreaming. But what would you do with all your beautiful things?'

'Supposing I sold it?'

'There I go again,' she said, all penitence. 'Of course you must keep it—it's such a perfect setting for them. We should only wreck it, shouldn't we, Harry?'

Embarrassed, he mumbled something.

My beautiful things! They had seemed so once, when one by one I had collected them: but how seldom had the glow of acquisition lasted from one side of the counter to the other! How soon one took them all for granted! Whereas the possessions of the mind!—It was the onset of old age, no doubt: once

I hadn't felt that way. Nor would a young couple coming fresh
to a place, with eyes and hearts alive to pretty things, feel that
way, either.

We were back in my study.

'Well, it has been a great experience,' said Sylvia, the spokes-
man of the two, 'a great privilege, and one we didn't deserve.
We ought to have been turned out on our ears. Instead, we've
had a glimpse of Paradise.'

'It's odd you should say that,' I said, 'for "Paradise Paddock" is the name of the house.'

'What an unusual name, and how appropriate! Thank you
so much, Mr. Minchin. Now Harry—'

She held her hand out, and I said:

'Just one more for the river?'

They laughed and Mr. Marchmont said: 'There's no law
against being drunk in charge of a boat.'

We drank, and his wife said: 'Here's good luck, Mr.
Minchin. You must never, never, never sell your house.'

The words struck my heart like a knell, and involuntarily I
said:

'Supposing I wanted to sell it, would you buy it?'

'But you don't want to sell it.'

'But if I did?'

The tension in my feelings must have spread to the room: it
seemed to listen for their answer.

'If you did, we should be buyers,' said Mr. Marchmont,
quietly. 'Provided, of course . . .'

'That we could afford it,' put in his wife.

I felt they could; you didn't buy a canoe to give away if you
were not well off.

'But where would you put all your lovely things?'

'They could go with the house.'

'Do you really mean that?' they asked me, almost in one
breath.

'I think I do, I think I do, I must have time to think,' I babbled.

'Of course you must, of course you must.' They looked at me with extreme concern, as if I had been taken ill: but hope and joy sparkled in their eyes.

'Imagine it,' said Mrs. Marchmont, rapt, ecstatic, as if she saw a vision. 'Imagine living here!'

More to gain time than for any other reason I said:

'Another for the river!'

But this time they refused.

'Two must be our limit.'

'Telephone me from your hotel when you get back,' I said, 'and I'll let you know, one way or the other.'

Their faces fell at the uncertainty, and my heart missed a beat. Could I draw back? Had I committed myself?

'I'll see you safely off the premises,' I said.

At that they smiled, and I smiled with them. But whereas I smiled in relief, that I could put off, for the moment, my decision, they smiled because their minds were made up, and they thought mine was, too. Victory! Paradise Paddock was within their grasp. It was slipping out of mine; was that defeat?

Twilight was falling when I escorted them to the landing-stage.

'Let me go first, the steps are a bit tricky here.'

When we were safely on the lawn I said:

'You ring me up—or shall I ring you?'

'Oh, we'll ring you up,' Mr. Marchmont said. 'You see we don't know when we shall be back.'

We had reached the second flight of steps, that led from the garden wall to the landing-stage.

'Oh look, the boat is still here!' cried Mrs. Marchmont.

'Why,' said her husband, 'did you think it would have floated away?'

'I have no faith in your knots,' his wife replied.

We laughed at this, no doubt thinking of the marriage knot. I bent down to steady the canoe: its satin-smooth surface pleased my fingers: I had little or no experience of canoes. Mrs. Marchmont lowered herself into the back seat; he scrambled into the front one. The paddles dipped and gleamed.

'But you are going the wrong way!'

They back-watered clumsily towards me.

'We thought we'd see a little more of the river,' he said.

'You won't find another house on it,' I warned them.

'We don't want to! We don't want to!'

'When you come by again on your way back, give me a shout,' I said, 'and I'll tell you what I've decided—if I've decided anything.'

'Please let it be yes!'

They tried to wave; the frail craft lurched and teetered, and they were off. It was only as I saw them disappearing, their white-clad figures shining on the shadowed water, their busy paddles digging puddles in it, that I was reminded of the swans.

Back at my writing-table on the terrace a black mood settled on me. I had had many such, sometimes without cause; but this one had a cause: the house itself was accusing me. Every window was an eye that looked reproach, a speaking eye that said, 'Why are you deserting me? You have been happy here, as happy as your temperament would let you be! It was love at first sight, wasn't it? Didn't you make your mind up, then and there, to buy me? And think of your joy when you took possessions—vacant possession as they called it, but it wasn't vacant, for I was here and I am still here, the genius loci, your tutelary god! You wrote round to all your friends, "Paradise Paddock is its name, and a veritable paradise it is!" How have I failed you? Why have you changed?'

I couldn't answer, and the voice went on, 'I'll tell you why you have turned against me—it's for the same reason that you took to me. You fell in love with me and now you've fallen in love with them—that couple that were here a moment ago. You'd never set eyes on them before but they took your fancy, just as I did, and you thought: "I can identify myself with them! Their youth shall be my youth, their happiness my happiness, their children my children, their future mine!" Yes, grey-haired Mr. Minchin, you thought you could renew yourself in them, and lead vicariously the life you never led! But I'm not so fickle! I don't want them and their squalling children, who will deafen me with their clamour and never listen to my voice as you did, till they came. I don't want them, I tell you, and what's more, I won't have them!'

The voice of jealousy, no doubt, piercing what seemed a lifetime of sad, conflicting thoughts; but I had to heed it, for I could feel the house's enmity like a cold air at my back, feel too the threat of imminent and lasting rupture that a quarrel with an old friend brings. I tried to stop my ears but still the voice droned on, painting my future life away from Paradise Paddock in hues as dark as my own thoughts, as dark as the shadows gathering on the river, where a patch of light under the low branches might have been a swan. And not only my future, but the house's too. For the Marchmonts wouldn't keep it, the voice told me. Was it likely that a whim, born of being in love, fostered by a fine evening and stimulated by two dry martinis (dry, mind you) for the river, would *last*? With the servant difficulty, and all those flights of stairs? Oh, no, mark my words, within a year, Paradise Paddock will again be on the market, and what then? A road-house, will it be, with the river-bank a lido? Or an old people's home, an eventide home—fast falls the eventide! Or gutted and converted into flats—homes for the homeless, but not a home for you, you will have no home. That precious word will have no meaning for you. You have given your home up to the Marchmonts.

·   ·   ·   ·   ·

It was then I heard the beating of the swan's wings, a unique sound, there is nothing like it, an aspirated gasping, as if the atmosphere itself was labouring to keep that mighty body airborne, fourteen pounds of bone and flesh and feathers, the heaviest living thing that flies. It chilled my blood, for to me it was the prelude to attack, the throbbing drone of the bombers before they loosed their bombs. I could see nothing on the shrouded river, but in my mind's eye I could see it all—the long white wings skimming towards me, and between them the bottle-shaped fuselage of body tapering to the arrowy neck and head—and, the next moment, crisis!—the necessity to think and act only in self-defence, to lose myself in anger, in mindless hostility, just as it, the swan, had.

But of course it wasn't me the bird was after: I was on dry land, out of harm's way. Its quarry now would be another swan—had been, perhaps, for this swan was a killer. Two or three times I'd seen a drifting body, its neck once white gnawed bare by rats or fishes. And when I reported this to the Inspector of the R.S.P.C.A., hoping to enlist his aid against the river tyrant, he only said, 'Yes, swans are like that.'

All this went through my mind, was driven into it by those powerful wing-beats, as if by a hammer.

When, a few seconds later, the sound ceased, the air was unburdened of its urgency, and so was I; I got up as easily as if no panic spell had bound me, and took a turn along the terrace. I was my own master again and the house beside me as sightless and as speechless as any other house. A respite, but only for a moment, and then I must decide, say yes or no, and not on grounds of sentiment or fantasy. Could I afford to keep the house? Not as it should be kept. Could the Marchmonts? Apparently they could. Should I find a buyer with more feeling for it and its genius loci (how that creature had bullied me!) than they had? No, I shouldn't. Then wasn't it more sensible to close with an offer which might not be repeated?

The answer must be yes.

I returned to my table on the terrace with my mind made up. Ignoring the foolscap that glimmered at me I let my elbows slide along the table and in a moment—I suppose it was the release from indecision—the darkness pressed down on my eyes and took me into it.

I dreamed and it was a dark dream, for the house was dark. I entered through the study door, but nowhere could I find the switch, and when at last I found it, it didn't work. This seemed to reinforce the darkness; I dared not move for fear of falling over something, and then I knew the house was hostile to me, something or someone didn't want me to come in. I was an outsider, but I couldn't get out any more than I could get in, for I couldn't tell where the door was. Where was I? If indoors, why did branches scrape against me? And what were these white flashes whirling round me, that clove the air like feathered scimitars? I tried to cry out but instead of my own voice I heard another, a jagged line of sound that struck against my ear and seemed to call my name. 'Mr. Minchin! Mr. Minchin!' The thin wail rose and fell. 'Remember to say yes,' I told myself. 'Yes is what you want and what they want. Yes, yes, yes, yes'—I was still saying it when I reached the river wall.

The sounds had stopped by then. Who knew how long the Marchmonts had been calling? Perhaps a long time; perhaps, getting no reply, they had given me up and were making tracks for Warmwell.

No, they were there, at least two people were who surely must be they—my visitors of who knew how long ago? My mind told me that they must be, though my eyes denied it, denied that this drenched couple in clothes no longer white but water-grey and so transparent that the skin showed through them, could be the Marchmonts. But their clothes were more recognizable than they were, for not a look I could remember, and hardly any awareness of themselves, each other, or of me, showed in their faces. The water in the canoe seemed to worry them, it was ankle-deep and they could not keep their feet still.

'You've had a spill,' I said. 'Come in and let me find you some dry clothes.'

Neither of them answered for a moment or two: Mrs. Marchmont was the first to find her tongue.

'No, thank you, we'll go on. We're not cold really. We shall be dry by the time we get to Warmwell. We stopped here because ... Why did we stop, Harry?'

'Because we said we would,' he answered in a voice of which the inflexions were quite out of his control. 'Mr. ... Mr. ... was going to tell us something.'

'Look, you've had a shock,' I said, 'a nasty experience. Do come in and I'll give you something to warm you.'

'We did have a nasty experience,' he said in his lilting sing-song. 'That's why we ... don't want to stay. That damned bird ... it set about us—'

'Ah,' I said, 'I was afraid so.'

'It got us in the water where the banks were high. I didn't think we could climb out, with it thrashing around. It got on to her back, the great big bugger, and would have drowned her, but I was on the bank by that time and I bashed it ... with the paddle, you know.'

'Did you kill it?' I asked.

'I think so. Do you see her dress, how torn it is, and her skin, all in ribbons. We'll have to see a doctor.'

I looked, and looked away.

'Yes,' I said, 'but do stay now. I'll call a doctor, if you like.'

He shook his head. 'We don't think the place is healthy for us, and we'd better be off, thanks all the same. And thanks for the drinks, too—what a big drink we nearly had! And thanks for everything. Now there was something we were going to tell you, or you were going to tell us, that's why we stopped. For the life of me, I can't think what it was.'

'It was about this house,' I said, 'Paradise Paddock. I was going to say that I would sell it if you wanted it.'

He laughed and laughed.

'Yes, that was it. What do you think, Sylvia, old girl?'

She shook her head and said, without looking up, and still twiddling her toes in the water, 'I'm afraid I don't want it now.'

'Don't think us rude, old chap,' her husband said, with sudden earnestness, 'but the fact is, we don't like your house any more. We think it's got a hoodoo on it. We don't want any more swan-songs.'

'I should feel the same,' I said, 'if I were you.' They shivered a little, and I shivered in concert.

'No offence meant, if we say we think this place is a bit lousy.'

'Of course not.'

'You find that it suits you?'

'Well, yes and no,' I said. 'It may suit me better now.' I was wondering if the swan was really dead.

'Well, thanks for all the drinks you gave us, thanks a lot.'

'Don't speak of it,' I said.

'We shall often think of you,' said Mrs. Marchmont suddenly, 'sitting and writing, with all your treasures round you.'

My heart sank, then soared.

'So you won't be settling in Warmwell?'

'Not on your life, not on your life ... Or ours,' he added. 'Excuse me—no offence intended.'

'I'm sorry about that,' I said. 'But you know best.' I saw that they were longing to be off, but didn't quite know how to take their leave.

'Let's tip the water out of the boat,' I suggested. 'You'll be more comfortable so.'

'Don't tip us out with it!'

'You'll have to debark first,' I said.

They laughed.

'We had forgotten that,' he said shakily.

When the operation was completed, and they were settled in again, he suddenly said: 'Would you accept this canoe as a memento, Mr. . . . Mr. . . . ?'

'Minchin,' put in his wife.

'Minchin, of course.'

'Most gratefully,' I said.

'I'll have it sent to Paradise Paddock, then . . .' He thought for a moment. 'Happy days,' he said. 'Have a good time,' said his wife, in an uncertain voice.

'And you!'

But they were already gone, and in a minute or two the darkness closed behind them.

I lingered by the river, trying to regain my faith in it, as one sometimes does with a friend after a quarrel. Mutely I apostrophized it. 'You have let me down, you have let me down! What have you to say?' But it was voiceless: the stealthy rustlings and stirring under the tree-laden banks were not meant for any ears, mine least of all. How vain to hope from nature a reciprocating mood, I thought—when suddenly, as though in answer to my thought, a V-shaped ripple stole along the river setting the water lapping at my feet, and after it a swan, a solitary swan. How changed she was! The anxious turning of the head from side to side, the questing, peering look, the jerky progress, that had lost its stately rhythm—they were quite unlike her; but most unlike was the little cry or call, louder than a moan, softer than a croak, that issued from her parted, yellow beak, which was so much less fearsome than his orange one.

She has never had to call for him before, I thought, and now he will not hear her.

There was nothing more to wait for; the air was turning cool; I had an irrational feeling that my clothes were wet.

Stiffly I got up and climbed back to the house—my house, for it was mine after all: the swan had saved it for me. A moment's doubt remained: would the switch work? It did, and showed me what was still my own.

Someone in the Lift

'THERE's someone coming down in the lift, Mummy!'

'No, my darling, you're wrong, there isn't.'

'But I can see him through the bars—a tall gentleman.'

'You think you can, but it's only a shadow. Now, you'll see, the lift's empty.'

And it always was.

This piece of dialogue, or variations of it, had been repeated at intervals ever since Mr. and Mrs. Maldon and their son Peter had arrived at the Brompton Court Hotel, where, owing to a domestic crisis, they were going to spend Christmas. New to hotel life, the little boy had never seen a lift before and he was fascinated by it. When either of his parents pressed the button to summon it he would take up his stand some distance away to watch it coming down.

The ground floor had a high ceiling so the lift was visible for some seconds before it touched floor level: and it was then, at its first appearance, that Peter saw the figure. It was always in the same place, facing him in the left-hand corner. He couldn't see it plainly, of course, because of the double grille, the gate of the lift and the gate of the lift-shaft, both of which had to be firmly closed before the lift would work.

He had been told not to use the lift by himself—an unnecessary warning, because he connected the lift with the things that grown-up people did, and unlike most small boys he wasn't over-anxious to share the privileges of his elders: he was content to wonder and admire. The lift appealed to him more as magic than as mechanism. Acceptance of magic made it possible for him to believe that the lift had an occupant when he first saw it, in spite of the demonstrable fact that when it came to rest, giving its fascinating click of finality, the occupant had disappeared.

'If you don't believe me, ask Daddy,' his mother said.

Peter didn't want to do this, and for two reasons, one of which was easier to explain than the other.

'Daddy would say I was being silly,' he said.

'Oh no, he wouldn't, he never says you're silly.'

This was not quite true. Like all well-regulated modern fathers, Mr. Maldon was aware of the danger of offending a son of tender years: the psychological results might be regrettable. But Freud or no Freud, fathers are still fathers, and sometimes when Peter irritated him Mr. Maldon would let fly. Although he was fond of him, Peter's private vision of his father was of someone more authoritative and awe-inspiring than a stranger, seeing them together, would have guessed.

The other reason, which Peter didn't divulge, was more fantastic. He hadn't asked his father because, when his father was with him, he couldn't see the figure in the lift.

Mrs. Maldon remembered the conversation and told her husband of it. 'The lift's in a dark place,' she said, 'and I dare say he does see something, he's so much nearer to the ground than we are. The bars may cast a shadow and make a sort of pattern that we can't see. I don't know if it's frightening him, but you might have a word with him about it.'

At first Peter was more interested than frightened. Then he began to evolve a theory. If the figure only appeared in his father's absence, didn't it follow that the figure might be, could be, must be, his own father? In what region of his consciousness Peter believed this it would be hard to say; but for imaginative purposes he did believe it and the figure became for him 'Daddy in the lift'. The thought of Daddy in the lift did frighten him, and the neighbourhood of the lift-shaft, in which he felt compelled to hang about, became a place of dread.

Christmas Day was drawing near and the hotel began to deck itself with evergreens. Suspended at the foot of the staircase, in front of the lift, was a bunch of mistletoe, and it was this that gave Mr. Maldon his idea.

As they were standing under it, waiting for the lift, he said to Peter:

'Your mother tells me you've seen someone in the lift who isn't there.'

His voice sounded more accusing than he meant it to, and Peter shrank.

'Oh, not now,' he said, truthfully enough. 'Only sometimes.'

'Your mother told me that you always saw it,' his father said, again more sternly than he meant to. 'And do you know who I think it may be?'

Caught by a gust of terror Peter cried, 'Oh, please don't tell me!'

'Why, you silly boy,' said his father reasonably. 'Don't you want to know?'

Ashamed of his cowardice, Peter said he did.

'Why, it's Father Christmas, of course!'

Relief surged through Peter.

'But doesn't Father Christmas come down the chimney?' he asked.

'That was in the old days. He doesn't now. Now he takes the lift!'

Peter thought a moment.

'Will you dress up as Father Christmas this year,' he asked, 'even though it's an hotel?'

'I might.'

'And come down in the lift?'

'I shouldn't wonder.'

After this Peter felt happier about the shadowy passenger behind the bars. Father Christmas couldn't hurt anyone, even if he was (as Peter now believed him to be) his own father. Peter was only six but he could remember two Christmas Eves when his father had dressed up as Santa Claus and given him a delicious thrill. He could hardly wait for this one, when the apparition in the corner would at last become a reality.

Alas, two days before Christmas Day the lift broke down. On every floor it served, and there were five (six counting the basement), the forbidding notice 'Out of Order' dangled from the door-handle. Peter complained as loudly as anyone, though secretly, he couldn't have told why, he was glad that the lift no longer functioned; and he didn't mind climbing the four flights to his room, which opened out of his parents' room but had its own door too. By using the stairs he met the workmen (he never knew on which floor they would be) and from them gleaned the latest news about the lift-crisis. They were working overtime, they told him, and were just as anxious as he to see the last of the job. Sometimes they even told each other to put a jerk into it. Always Peter asked them when they would be finished, and they always answered, 'Christmas Eve at latest.'

Peter didn't doubt this. To him the workmen were infallible, possessed of magic powers capable of suspending the ordinary laws that governed lifts. Look how they left the gates open, and shouted to each other up and down the awesome lift-shaft, paying as little attention to the other hotel visitors as if they didn't exist! Only to Peter did they vouchsafe a word.

But Christmas Eve came, the morning passed, the afternoon passed, and still the lift didn't go. The men were working with set faces and a controlled hurry in their movements; they didn't even return Peter's 'Good night' when he passed them on his way to bed. Bed! He had begged to be allowed to stay up this once for dinner; he knew he wouldn't go to sleep, he said, till Father Christmas came. He lay awake, listening to the urgent voices of the men, wondering if each hammer-stroke would be the last; and then, just as the clamour was subsiding, he dropped off.

Dreaming, he felt adrift in time. Could it be midnight? No, because his parents had after all consented to his going down to dinner. Now was the time. Averting his eyes from the for-bidden lift he stole downstairs. There was a clock in the hall, but it had stopped. In the dining-room there was another clock; but dared he go into the dining-room alone, with no one to guide him and everybody looking at him?

He ventured in, and there, at their table, which he couldn't always pick out, he saw his mother. She saw him, too, and came towards him, threading her way between the tables as if they were just bits of furniture, not alien islands under hostile sway.

'Darling,' she said, 'I couldn't find you—nobody could, but here you are!' She led him back and they sat down. 'Daddy will be with us in a minute.' The minutes passed; suddenly there was a crash. It seemed to come from within, from the kitchen perhaps. Smiles lit up the faces of the diners. A man at a near-by table laughed and said, 'Something's on the floor! Somebody'll be for it!' 'What is it?' whispered Peter, too excited to speak out loud. 'Is anyone hurt?' 'Oh, no, darling, somebody's dropped a tray, that's all.'

To Peter it seemed an anti-climax, this paltry accident that had stolen the thunder of his father's entry, for he didn't doubt that his father would come in as Father Christmas. The sus-pense was unbearable. 'Can I go into the hall and wait for him?' His mother hesitated and then said yes.

The hall was deserted, even the porter was off duty. Would it be fair, Peter wondered, or would it be cheating and doing himself out of a surprise, if he waited for Father Christmas by the lift? Magic has its rules which mustn't be disobeyed. But he was there now, at his old place in front of the lift; and the lift would come down if he pressed the button.

He knew he mustn't, that it was forbidden, that his father would be angry if he did; yet he reached up and pressed it.

But nothing happened, the lift didn't come, and why? Because some careless person had forgotten to shut the gates— 'monkeying with the lift', his father called it. Perhaps the workmen had forgotten, in their hurry to get home. There was only one thing to do—find out on which floor the gates had been left open, and then shut them.

On their own floor it was, and in his dream it didn't seem strange to Peter that the lift wasn't there, blocking the black hole of the lift-shaft, though he daren't look down it. The gates clicked to. Triumph possessed him, triumph lent him wings; he was back on the ground floor, with his finger on the button. A thrill of power such as he had never known ran through him when the machinery answered to his touch.

But what was this? The lift was coming up from below, not down from above, and there was something wrong with its roof—a jagged hole that let the light through. But the figure was there in its accustomed corner, and this time it hadn't disappeared, it was still there, he could see it through the mazy criss-cross of the bars, a figure in a red robe with white fur edges, and wearing a red cowl on its head: his father, Father Christmas, Daddy in the lift. But why didn't he look at Peter, and why was his white beard streaked with red?

The two grilles folded back when Peter pushed them. Toys were lying at his father's feet, but he couldn't touch them for they too were red, red and wet as the floor of the lift, red as the jag of lightning that tore through his brain . . . .

The Face

EDWARD POSTGATE was a one-woman man. Or perhaps it would be truer to say, he was a man to whom one facial type appealed. He wasn't singular in this, for most men have their favourite type. But he was singular in the fact that no other type, or even variation of his own type, seemed to attract him at all. Long before he married Mary Elmhirst, this type was enshrined in his consciousness and most of his friends knew what it was. Not because he told them; he was reserved about such matters, and his marriage, when it came, was a surprise. But the girl's face was not a surprise, for anyone who had done examinations with him or played bridge with him, or sat with him at a committee or a board meeting, could not help knowing it. He was an inveterate doodler. Sometimes he covered the margin with abstract designs; sometimes with plumes and feathers (he was especially fond of drawing ostrich feathers), but most often it was a face, and it was always the same face, recognizably the same, from whatever angle he drew it. The back view was particularly characteristic, for the girl of his dreams, unlike girls in real life, always did her hair the same way—in a knob low down on her neck. Edward was enough of a draughtsman to be able to show that her hair was dark and shining, her eyes violet blue, her colouring red and white —almost a deep red on the high cheek-bones. Parted in the middle, her hair swept round a broad forehead, and was drawn back, but not pulled back, to emphasize the slightly concave line that led from her cheek-bones to her small round chin. However many curves he gave her mouth, it was always a wide one, otherwise her nose, whose low arch made a curve that didn't vary, might have looked too large.

'There's that girl again!' we sometimes said, and hardier spirits even said to Edward: 'Why don't you try another type for a change?' Whereat he would smile and sometimes scrunch the paper up. Many of us thought that he was in love with an ideal, a Dulcinea who, unlike Don Quixote's, never had and never would exist in real life: she was an alibi for feelings that he only had on paper. Not that he avoided women's society — he was attached to several, and they to him; but in his relations with them there was a marked absence of the obsessiveness that showed so clearly in the drawings; he scarcely seemed to prefer one to another, nor did any of them resemble, even remotely, the face he loved to contemplate.

Edward was a well-built, fair-skinned man, with pale-green hair and amber eyes — at least they said so, I couldn't quite see it. To me he was self-coloured — not in the sense of being an egotist, he was anything but that — but he had no light and shade: he presented a uniform hue, the neutral hue of a good fellow. One didn't have to like him first to find him likeable; he was likeable at once. Many a hostess finding herself a man short used to say, 'Can't we get hold of that miserable Edward?' — only to find that another hostess had got hold of him. In company he always seemed to be holding himself back, as if he had something he didn't want to part with; it was the energy, I suppose, that he needed for his paper-mistress — his drawing-mistress, as we sometimes called her.

So his marriage, at the age of twenty-eight, came as a great surprise. Mary Elmhirst didn't belong to any of the circles he frequented, he ran into her at some seaside town, and they were married almost at once. The match was suitable in every way; she was a doctor's daughter, at once gay and serious-minded; he worked in the City. As a bachelor he had been a social asset and in continuous demand at parties. As a married man he didn't exactly drop out, but he would go nowhere without his wife; he ceased being Edward, he became Edward and Mary, or perhaps Mary and Edward. In the social and every other sense he lived entirely for her, and it then became more than ever apparent how superficial his previous friendships had been. We accepted this with a smile and a shrug; a few tried, and one or two pretended to find, rifts in the Postgates' matrimonial lute, but these were so obviously unfounded that they passed into a joke, a joke against the gossips. Happy the couple that has no history, but also the less interesting: Mary and Edward, whether meaning one or both of them, ceased to be names that came up much in conversation, and where they did, it was chiefly as types of conjugal felicity. Nothing more would happen to them except a child, and this, strangely enough, they did not have, though they were going to have one when five years later Mary Postgate was killed in a motor accident.

It was like a looking-glass being broken—the picture was no longer there, nor did the fragments that remained present any coherent pattern. What had happened to Edward? What was happening? What would happen? It was anybody's guess, and meanwhile, after the letters of condolence sometimes easy to write but in this case next to impossible, we were in a state of suspense and bewilderment, unable when with Edward, or even apart from him, to decide whether 'yes' or 'no' was the more appropriate word. Did he prefer to see people, or not to see them? Was it better to refer to his loss, or not to refer to it? One felt that he, too, was dead, had died when all he stood for died; but he wasn't, he was up and going about; and if we could find some definite mode or pattern of thinking and feeling about him, it might help him to find one for himself. Perhaps he had found one, but if so he didn't disclose it. He withdrew further into his pre-marital reserve. That he was still attending to his business, and wasn't actively ill, at any rate physically, was all we knew with certainty about him. After a while he began to move about a little socially, he returned to circulation; but he didn't function as a person, he was like a clock that people still look at even though it has stopped.

Everyone of course was sorry for him, I not least, being one of his oldest friends, and a born bachelor, as he had seemed to be—though not with the facial attachment that he had. I would say to him: 'Edward, come in for a drink on Thursday —I'm having a few friends,' and as like as not he would accept, and yet he might as well have stayed away, for he didn't bring himself with him, not even the muted self we used to know. We were sorry for him, I repeat, but you can't feel the pang of sorrow indefinitely: the nerve gets overlaid and ceases to respond. He was still a charge on our feelings—'Poor Edward!'—but he was no longer news.

And then somebody remarked, who had been with him at a meeting, that he had started to draw the face again. All the years that he was married, and for some years after, he hadn't drawn it. Possessing it he hadn't needed to, and losing it he hadn't the heart to—at least this was the explanation generally given. The face, so my informant told me, and this was soon confirmed by others who had seen it in other versions, was still the same face, hadn't altered in any particular—it was even the same age it used to be. I felt a little sceptical about these rumours, but one evening, when I was playing cards with him, I saw it myself, decorating the bridge-marker. Time, as someone said of Dr. Johnson, had given him a younger wife. But was she still his old wife, Mary, or a potential new wife? Or just his obsession with his ideal?

Nothing happened for a long time, and then a mutual friend called Thomas Henry told me that at a café in Restbourne where he was having tea he had been served by a waitress, whose face was the facsimile of Edward's model, the spitting image, he said. Thomas Henry was a fussy little man, twice married, and as meddlesome as a woman; he was fond of starting hares, especially matrimonial hares, for other people to follow up. Now he was all agog. 'But what can we do about it?' I asked him.

'Well, bring them together.'

'But how?'

'Tell him to go down to the café and see for himself.'

I deprecated this—it seemed too crude.

'We don't know how he feels,' I said. 'It might upset him terribly—you can't monkey about with people's emotions in that way.'

'All the same,' said Thomas Henry, 'it might be the saving of him and bring him back to life, and think how nice for her!' That aspect of the case hadn't occurred to me, nor, I must say, did it appeal to me. A waitress in a café! Without being a snob I thought it most unsuitable, and said so. 'Why,' said Thomas Henry, 'you old diehard, we live in a classless society, or soon shall, and all he cares about is the Face. He doesn't care about anything else.'

'Oh, nonsense,' I said, 'he's an idealist through and through. It wasn't just chance that Mary was as nice as she was nice-looking. The Face is the face of a lady— Besides, it may not be his face—the face he thinks about—at all. We've only your word for it.'

'Well, go and see for yourself,' he said.

It happened to be very inconvenient for me to do this, and besides, I didn't want to spend the day going to Restbourne, just to have tea and come back. And what a wild-goose chase! I was Edward's age, nearly forty, and doing things I didn't like was becoming increasingly hard for me. Self-discipline is all right for the young, but for those of riper years it is just another brake on the already overclogged machinery of living. All the same, for the sake of my old friendship with Edward I decided to go to Restbourne and inspect the waitress.

I saw her the moment I got inside the Krazie Café, and seeing her I saw what Thomas Henry meant. I hovered, looking for a table at which she would be serving; luckily she came up to me and showed me one. I scrutinized her as she stood waiting for my order. Yes—the resemblance was most striking —even to the deeper colour on the high cheek-bones—though that, perhaps, owed something to art, for she was more made-up than Mary had been. Her voice was made up too; it had an obvious overlay of gentility but Edward didn't draw voices. I called her back to ask her for some jam; the hands that brought it were innocent of a wedding-ring: they were larger than Mary's, and not so pretty, but Edward didn't draw hands. What was she like in herself? Like Mary? How could I tell? She didn't chat much to the other customers, and they paid her no special attention. How tantalizing it was! Before I left I must say something to her—something to draw her out. But I was hopeless at that sort of thing: I hadn't the right touch: least of all the light touch. I couldn't leave it to the moment of settling the bill; at the risk of being a nuisance I must again ask for something. But how could I, when the table was groaning with food and I never ate tea anyway? Distaste for my mission increased: I longed to get it over. Never a chatterbox myself, the waitress seemed the last person in the world I wished to talk to. I must; but not at the cost of eating my way through all those viands. Hastily pouring all the hot water into the teapot, I caught her eye.

'Some more hot water, please,' I said, forbiddingly.

When she brought it she said: 'Why, you are thirsty!'

I didn't like her familiarity but it broke the ice.

'Do you know,' I said, 'you remind me of someone I used to know.'

'Somebody nice?' she asked.

'Er . . . very nice.'

'And were you thinking I might do instead?'

It was what I was thinking, but not in the sense that she meant. Instantly I decided that she would not do, but that I ought to give her another chance. Besides, there was something else I wanted her to tell me.

Ignoring her question I said: 'She might have been your twin, she was so like you. . . . Her name was Mary Elmhirst.'

'I have a twin sister as it happens,' she said, 'and she's very like me, except she dresses differently, more of a mouse, you know, and doesn't wear much make-up. Otherwise people couldn't tell us apart, we're always being mistaken for each other—it's quite inconvenient at times. I'm Doris—Doris Blackmore—no relation to your friend, I'm afraid. I hope you're not disappointed.'

I answered at random: 'No, of course not. But it gave me a slight shock, I mean the likeness did.'

'Someone you were fond of?'

'The wife of a friend of mine.'

'Oh, I'm sorry.'

Whatever she meant by that, I liked her better for saying it.

'Well,' I said, 'I must be off.'

'But you haven't drunk your hot water. I don't believe you really wanted it. You just wanted to—'

'You don't make an extra charge for hot water, do you?' I interrupted.

She laughed.

'I make an extra charge for talking. I don't talk to many of our customers.'

'No?'

'No. They want to start something funny with me, the men do. I thought that you—'

'No,' I assured her. 'It was just the likeness.'

She looked disappointed.

'Oh well, then, if you don't—'

'But I've enjoyed it,' I said firmly, 'all the same.'

'A bit lonely, are you?'

'I suppose we all are, at times. Look, there's somebody wants you.'

She turned her head. 'I see that you don't,' she said, walking away with exaggerated slowness.

I thought, 'You impudent hussy,' but I didn't feel as annoyed as I'd expected to. When she had attended to the other customer she came back.

'I suppose you want your bill.'

'Yes, please.'

She made it out and handed it to me.

'Do you generally talk that way to girls?'

'Oh no,' I said, fumbling in my pocket, 'I'm like you, I hardly talk to anyone.'

'Pay at the desk, please,' she said, looking sullen.

I laid a shilling on the table.

'All right, but that's for you.'

'I don't know that I want to take it,' she said. 'You haven't much respect for a girl's feelings, have you?'

Angry tears stood in her dark-blue eyes. I was amazed and jumped up from the table. The bill paid, I walked past her to say goodbye, but she took no notice of me.

'I saw what you meant,' I said to Thomas Henry for the third time. (I had edited the story, leaving out the last part.) 'It's an unbelievable likeness. But she wouldn't do at all. She's utterly unsuitable.' I had said this three times too.

'All the same, I think we ought to tell him.'

'But why? Nothing would come of it, or at any rate, nothing but harm.'

'I think we owe it to him.'

'An item for his experience account? No, really, Thomas

Henry. Besides, how could we bring the subject up? I've never heard him mention Mary since she died, and I've never dared to mention her to him. The wound went much too deep. You never know what's going on in people's minds. The idea of another woman looking like her might upset him terribly, and destroy whatever compromise he's been able to make with himself and life about her. We know he's made one, because he still functions like an ordinary person. This might upset the balance and then God knows what would happen.'

'He still draws the Face.'

'Yes, but we don't know why. It's probably just to keep Mary's image in his mind. It would be tasteless and tactless beyond belief to suggest to him that he might be interested in another woman, and above all that woman.'

'You yourself didn't seem to dislike her all that much.'

'I? My dear fellow, I was amused by the whole episode, but only because there was a time limit to it. If I'd had to spend another five minutes in her company I should have died.'

'You never liked the company of women very much.'

'Well, not women of that type.'

'That's for him to decide. The point is, we must give him the chance. With Mary he was blissfully happy. He fulfilled himself in her. He lives for one person; the rest of us are shadows. Now he's emotionally mutilated—paralysed. If you could see the emptiness of his life—'

'I can't, and nor can you.'

'—you'd realize that anything is better than the void, *le néant*. You've never been attached to anyone—'

'How do you know?'

'Isn't it obvious? You're quite self-sufficient. Whereas he—'

'Well, I'm not going to tell him.'

'Then I shall. But first let me get it right. She works in Restbourne, at the Krazie Café, and her name is—'

'I've forgotten.'

B*

'But you knew it a moment ago.'

'Well, I've forgotten now. And I beg you, Thomas Henry, not to tell him anything about her. I beseech you—'

'All right, I won't bring you into it—'

'For God's sake don't.'

'And I'll take all the blame and all the credit, too, if it comes off.'

'If what comes off?'

'Well, if the Face fits.'

When I next saw Thomas Henry, some days later, it was in the company of other people, and we hardly spoke. I knew I was avoiding him, and I thought he was avoiding me: but why? Edward I did see to pass the time of day with: and to my surprise I found myself asking him to lunch with me.

'What about next Saturday?'

'Let me get my little book,' he said. 'I'm afraid I'm engaged on Saturday.'

'Well, the following Saturday?' He turned the leaves.

'I'm engaged then, too. Silly, isn't it?'

'I know you can't get away easily in the middle of the week,' I said, 'but what about Wednesday?'

'I'm not quite sure about Wednesday,' he hedged. 'I'll let you know.'

'Don't let me be a nuisance,' I said, 'but it would be nice to see you. You lunch out sometimes, Edward, don't you?'

'Oh yes,' he said with his polite air that kept one at a distance, 'but just at this moment I seem to have more engagements than usual. I'll tell you about Wednesday.'

A day or two later he telephoned that he couldn't manage it. I was unaccountably disappointed, for much as I liked Edward I had never set great store on seeing him.

The next time I met Thomas Henry was at a cocktail party, and this time I didn't let him escape me. 'What about

Edward?' I asked. 'Did you tell him about our friends at Restbourne?' I used the plural as a precaution: friends sounded less compromising than friend. But he looked round apprehensively and said, 'Not here, I think. Stone walls—'

'No one else can hear you,' I said, shouting above the din. 'I can hardly hear you myself.' When he still wouldn't be drawn I pinned him down to dinner the next day.

A strange tale he told me. He was unhappy about it, as he should have been, and very much on the defensive.

'I couldn't have guessed what would happen,' he said. 'I acted for the best.'

'No one does so much harm as those who go about doing good,' I said, quoting Bishop Creighton.

'You never run that risk,' he retorted tartly.

'Well, not on this occasion, perhaps,' I answered, 'and I warned you not to.' Realizing we were on the verge of a quarrel, and I might get no more out of him, I succeeded in pacifying him: few things make one angrier with other people than being angry with oneself.

He had been playing bridge with Edward and seen the face appearing on the bridge-marker. He made no comment at the time, but when Edward was giving him a lift home he plucked up courage and said he had seen a girl whose face reminded him of the face Edward had been drawing—he didn't say it reminded him of Mary, and now I come to think of it, I don't believe any of Edward's friends had ever remarked to him on the resemblance, though they often spoke of it to each other. Edward said: 'Oh, have you?' and the car swerved a bit. Then Edward asked him where he had seen her, and Thomas Henry told him, but couldn't tell him her name because I had forgotten it.

'You didn't tell him that?' I asked.

'Oh, no. I left you out of it, as I promised to.'

Then Thomas Henry asked if he would be interested in seeing her, and Edward said he wasn't sure; he said the drawings were a vice which he had given up when he was married. He said this in quite an ordinary tone and changed the subject. But when he next saw Thomas Henry he told him he had been down to Restbourne.

'Oh!' I said.

'Yes, but the bird had flown. There was no one in the café in the least resembling her. He went to Restbourne three Saturdays running, and twice in the middle of the week, making some excuse of going on business—five times altogether, but he never saw her.'

'She might have been away on holiday,' I said, 'on those three Saturdays. It's August.'

'I suggested that,' said Thomas Henry, 'and he's going to try again. He would have asked about her, but he couldn't, not knowing her name.'

'Did he seem upset?' I asked.

'He certainly couldn't talk of anything else.'

'Look what you've done, Thomas Henry! You can't say you weren't warned.'

'No, but it may have given him an object in life. He was much more animated than he used to be.'

The next time we met, Thomas Henry was less optimistic. 'He's been down there again,' he said, without bothering to explain who 'he' was, 'and she isn't there. He told me he thought I'd made a mistake, because he wasn't a good draughtsman, and what he drew corresponded to something inside him, not outside (he didn't mention Mary). He said that each line had a special meaning for him, and any deviation from it, in a human face, made that face quite unlike the face of his conception. And yet he couldn't help thinking that I might be right, and that one day she might come back, and he

would find her. "She may be ill," he said, "or one of her relations may be ill. In the working-classes, some relation or other
is nearly always ill"—you know the way he talks about the
working-classes, as if they were another type of human being.'

'They are,' I said.

'Oh, nonsense. But I do think we should do something for
him—he can't go on like this, commuting between here and
Restbourne like a . . . like a . . .'

'Shuttle on a loom,' I said. 'Well, you do something,
Thomas Henry, it's your pigeon. Vous l'avez voulu, Georges
Dandin.'

'Yes, I felt for him more than you did. I saw a fellow
creature suffering, and wanted to relieve him. Whereas you—'

'Passed by on the other side.'

'It's nothing to be proud of. But now you can do something
to rid him of his obsession. You can go down to Restbourne,
Ernest, and find out what's happened to her.'

'Why not you? I'm not specially keen on the south coast in
August.'

'Because you talked to her, and made yourself conspicuous,
as no doubt they all remember in the café. You might even
pose as a relation.'

'Thank you,' I said. 'One of the sick ones, perhaps.'

'Oh, do go, Ernest. You're a man of independent means.
It's much easier for you. You don't have to be in any special
place at any special time, so why not go to Restbourne?'

'Restbourne is the last place I want to go to,' I replied. But
in the end I went.

The appalling vulgarity of that town! Nowhere has the
proletarianization of the English race gone so fast, or so far, as
it has at Restbourne. It is the apotheosis of the synthetic. I
dreaded it, and when I got there it was worse than I remembered—an exhibition of what was, to my middle-class mind, a
substitute for every form of pleasure. Not that it was not

expensive, for it was; everyone seemed to have money to burn. But how joyless that sometimes gay proceeding made them! How they trailed about on the sea-front, well fed, well dressed (so far as they were dressed), well tanned, well oiled (sometimes in both senses of the word), but among the lot not one whom a photographer, still less a biographer, would ever want to make his subject.

It was a relief to sit down in the Krazie Café, for a chair is a chair, and tiredness is tiredness, whatever a mass-produced consciousness may have done to take the reality out of most objects and sensations. She wasn't there, Doris Blackmore wasn't there: I saw that at a glance; and the full weight of five hours thrown away, and five pounds thrown away on railway-trains and taxis, fell on me so crushingly that I groaned aloud. And sharpening my general disappointment was a particular one which I couldn't or wouldn't account for then. Deep down in me I had hoped to see the waitress. Why? To bandy words with her? To let her know where she got off, or didn't get off? I couldn't tell. But my sense of grievance was so overwhelming and acute that I did what, coming down in the train, I hadn't thought possible—for me, at any rate. With a clear conscience, which for some reason mine wasn't, it should have been quite easy; just a few words, casually uttered, as if the inquiry was the most natural in the world, and the thing would have been done. But in the train, however often I rehearsed them, whatever accent of indifference I gave them, they would not pass my lips. Now I knew they would, and when I had paid my bill I went up to the woman who seemed to be in charge and said:

'Can you tell me what's become of the waitress, Doris Blackmore I think her name was, who used to be here?'

At that the woman's face stiffened and she said shortly:

'I'm afraid I can't. She left us at a few days' notice. Naturally, we did not pay her her week's wages.'

'How long ago was that?'

'Over a month, I think. She said she was fed up, and she was earning good money, too. They're all alike—you can't rely on them. A whim, a fancied slight, a boy, you never know what it is, and then they're off.'

'A pity,' I said. 'She seemed to be a nice girl.'

The manageress pursed her lips and shrugged.

'No nicer than the rest. They're spoilt, if you ask me.'

'And you don't know where she's gone?'

'I'm sorry, but I can't help you.'

Well, that was that. My next step was to tell Thomas Henry (who was going to pretend that he had made the journey down to Restbourne) to tell Edward that the Face had been, well, effaced. Useless to look for it; better forget about it. And this he did, assuring Edward, who didn't want to be convinced, that any further raids on Restbourne would be fruitless. Fruitless for me, too, I reflected. The incident rankled like a sore place that hurts and is desired, as Cleopatra said, not only for its own sake but for the contrast with the healthy tissues round it.

At that time I had a flat in Knightsbridge overlooking Hyde Park and it was my nightly custom, for the sake of my health, to take a brisk constitutional in the Park before retiring. Between Hyde Park Corner and Wellington Barracks was my usual beat, but it was not only my beat, I shared it with a great many others who were not there for their health. Some sat, some stood, some walked, some drove up or drove away in motor-cars that seemed to hug the kerbstone in a peculiarly intimate manner and in some way—perhaps by exuding a moral cloud—to darken the surrounding air. I won't say anything against them for fear I should offend the live-and-let-live spirit of high-minded persons; but walking by them I had to run a gauntlet of hullos, dearies, darlings, and other forms of affectionate solicitation, and I got very tired of it. Indeed, but for a certain obstinacy, and the feeling that the Park was mine as well as theirs, I should have bent my steps another way.

When accosted I had not, as some men have, a polite formula of refusal ready: I swerved or dodged or walked straight on. But one evening I couldn't, for my solicitrix, who had risen from a seat a few yards farther on, planted herself in front of me and blocked my way.

'Hello, darling,' she said.

If her face hadn't been almost touching mine I should have recognized her sooner. If I had been less put out I should have recognized her sooner.

'Doris Blackmore!' I said at last.

'The same,' she answered. 'I've seen you several times doing your nightly dozen, or whatever you were here for, so I thought, "Why not me as well as one of the others?"'

'I don't come here to pick up women,' I said.

'I thought not, but one can't be sure, I haven't had much experience you see. Even the older ones can't always tell.'

'They can't, indeed,' I said.

'No need to be snooty. You might be wanting something—other men do.'

I made no answer.

'Do you know,' she said, 'yours is the first face I've recognized since I've been on the game.'

'On the game?'

'Well, on the batter, hustling, there are lots of names for it.'

'I could say the same,' I said. 'Yours is the first face that I've recognized among your crowd.'

'You're one of the lucky ones,' she told me, without rancour. 'You can pick and choose, whereas we— Well, so long. Nice to have seen you.'

She was strutting off, with that peculiar stiff gait they all affect, when I caught her up.

'Why on earth are you doing this?' I asked.

'Oh, I dunno. It's a break, at any rate. I got browned off at Restbourne. After you came—"

'Yes?' I said.

'Well, I just felt I wanted to do something else. That's all there is to it.'

'You'll get browned off doing this.'

'There's more variety and much more money, too. Some of us make forty pounds a week. I'd sooner go the whole way with somebody than natter with them at a tea-table. Some men think they're men just because they've been accosted. Some just come to look at us. We're not all so bad. I've heard of a Tom who blew a policeman's whistle for him when he'd been kicked in the groin and couldn't move.'

'I wasn't criticizing you,' I said, 'or them.'

'It's not a bad life. Most men are all mouth and trousers— well, I like the trousers best, if you see what I mean.'

'You mean without the trousers.'

'Yes, I suppose I do. Well, bye-bye, Mr. So-and-so. You didn't tell me your name. London's such a big place. It's nice to think we're neighbours.'

'Look here,' I said.

'I can't afford to waste another minute. Big Harry will be after me.'

'Are you here every night?'

'Yes, till they send me somewhere else.'

'Goodbye, good luck,' I said, and shook her hand. 'Perhaps I shall be seeing you.'

As a rule, on my nightly rambles, my thoughts follow their own course. But this time they wouldn't, they kept returning to the problem of Doris and Edward, digging straight lines from me to them, making an angle which, when I came into it, assumed the dignity and completeness of a triangle.

But I didn't come into it much. The wave of tenderness I

had felt for Doris the waitress didn't reach to Doris the whore; I could only see her as a member of her profession, for which I felt no sentiment at all. An uneasiness, a twinge of guilt I did feel, wondering if my visit to Restbourne, and the kindness I hadn't meant to show her, had been the last straw which broke the back of her virtue—if she was virtuous then.

But Edward, that unknown quantity, would he mind what her calling was, if she had the face he dreamed about? Like most of his circle, Edward was well off. It was taken for granted that any of us had unlimited supplies of gin and vermouth, or whatever drink was in favour at the moment. He had dropped some money over his marriage, for the settlement he had made on Mary came back to him at her death much reduced, when the Inland Revenue had had their whack. More than once, in expansive moments, he had praised the wisdom of parting with one's money in one's lifetime—at which some people pricked up their ears. 'But,' he said, 'most of my friends are my own age, and better off than I am, so where would be the point? I must give some of myself with the gift, or it's no fun; and nearly everyone I know has much more personality than I have—they couldn't do with more.' So it became a sort of game to find for Edward a possible legatee, and many very odd ones were suggested, though not, of course, to him. He was right about his lack of personality; he was more real when he was being talked about than when he was present. He used to say his friends invented him. But the current of his being flowed in a secret channel invisible to us.

Of all the suggested recipients of his bounty none was quite so fantastic as Doris Blackmore. Yet was she really so unsuitable? Besides having the Face, hadn't she almost all the qualifications, including lack of personality? Having been all things to all men, she might find it the less difficult to be one thing to one.

'Edward,' I said, one evening when we were together, 'excuse the question, but have you ever been with a prostitute?'

He frowned, and fixed his amber eyes on me.

'Why, no,' he said.

'Does the thought of them repel you?'

'I've never given them much thought.'

'Nor had I until a night or two ago when one accosted me in the Park, and do you know, she rather took my fancy.'

'Did you get off with her?' asked Edward.

'Well, no, it isn't in my line. But I talked to her and found her interesting and sympathetic. Does that shock you?'

'Not in the least,' said Edward. 'I'm not shocked by sexual irregularities or even'—he smiled—'by sexual regularity.'

'Would you care to meet her?'

'Not in the street, perhaps.'

'No, at some restaurant. She wouldn't look different from other girls—I'd see to that.'

'Very well,' he said. 'But can she get away? I mean, their bosses keep them pretty hard at work.'

'I'd give her something she could show for herself.'

'Well, let me in on that. What do you think—a fiver?'

But when I told her that a friend was going to join us, she seemed disappointed.

'I thought it was only you,' she said.

'Only me? You're not flattering,' I said. 'But yes, you are. Still, this friend of mine, he's a nice fellow, and of course I need a chaperon.'

'I should have thought you were old and ugly enough to look after yourself.'

'That's where you're wrong. At my age I can't afford to take risks.'

'I suppose you want me to get off with him?'

'Good lord!' I said. 'But if I did, would you object?'

'Object?' she repeated. 'Girls like me can't afford to object to anything.'

'Oh, come,' I rallied her. 'Your life is one long record of objections—all that I know of it, which isn't much. You objected to the Krazie Café; you objected to being talked to, you objected to not being talked to—'

'Only because you were so inconsiderate.'

'Inconsiderate?'

'All right,' she said, 'I'll come.'

Doris's conversation wasn't dull—at least not dull to me— but it was limited. She liked it to be a sparring match; she also peppered it with catch-words of the day—euphemisms and verbal subterfuges. 'Fair enough' for something that wasn't quite fair; 'Jolly good' to make something sound jollier and better than it was; and 'All right' with an interrogative inflexion to cover something that was not quite all right.

But we were both handicapped. We waited and waited, she and I, churning out gobbets of small talk. Conversation always becomes difficult between two people who are waiting for a third who doesn't come. The flow of communication is held up by the mere fact that at any moment it may be broken; and a kind of suspense starts which paralyses the tongue. I seized the opportunity to sing Edward's praises: he was the most amiable of men and the soul of punctuality. This sounded a little hollow in view of his manifest unpunctuality, and Doris, who was looking very pretty and anything but tartish, said:

'I suppose he doesn't want to meet somebody like me. Fair enough.'

'Oh, no,' I said. 'He was most anxious to meet you. He's not a man with silly prejudices and besides—' my voice trailed away under the accusing eye of the clock, which said eight-thirty. An invitation to dinner—eight-thirty for eight! One could tease him about that.

'I don't think much of a man who says he'll dine out with a prostitute,' said Doris unexpectedly. 'No nice man would.'

'What about me?'

'Oh, you're different. He's thought better of it, you can bet your life, and I don't blame him.'

'It's not like him to be late.'

'So you keep saying. I expect it's not like him to be dining with somebody like me.'

'Don't keep saying that—you're not like anyone except yourself.'

'All he wants is to go to bed with me.'

'A moment ago you were saying that he wouldn't come because you were a—'

'That's right, try to make me contradict myself.'

'Mr. Lenthall, please, Mr. Lenthall, please,' intoned a page-boy in a high-pitched nasal sing-song, threading his way between the tables, fixing each guest in turn with a speculative, hopeful stare. 'A telephone call for Mr. Lenthall, please. Mr. Lenthall, please.'

It was only when he had called my name for the fourth time that I realized he meant me.

'Excuse me,' I said, rising.

'Is that your name? You never told me. You never tell me anything.'

I didn't like to leave her to herself—I had a vague idea that the other diners might rise and drum her out—but I was glad to get away. As a companion, the telephone made less demands than Doris.

'Is that Ernest?'

'Yes, you old devil. Why aren't you here? Where are you?'

'At Restbourne.'

'Where?'

'At Restbourne.'

The story he told me didn't to me make sense. I had to believe it because Edward was nothing if not truthful, but believing it I also had to doubt my sanity. The telephone-box became a cage, a padded cell.

'You can't mean that.'

'But I do mean it. I'm terribly sorry, but you do understand, don't you? Make what excuses for me you can.'

'I don't understand a single thing, so how can I make excuses for you?'

'Tell her what I've told you.'

'I can't explain why now, but she won't believe it any more than I do—not so much. She'll have a special reason for not believing it. She'll scratch my eyes out—you don't know what women of that sort can do.'

'Tell her it was love at first sight. She must be used to that.'

'To lust no doubt, but not to love. You are a brute, letting me down like this. And I don't believe you're in Restbourne at all, you're here, in the next room.'

Edward laughed. His happiness had made him pachydermatous. He kept saying he was sorry, but not a trace of shame showed in his voice. It was so full of triumph and personal elation that I hardly recognized it.

'Are you spending the night at Restbourne?'

'Yes, and perhaps tomorrow night. I must ring off now—she's waiting for me.'

'Well,' said Doris. 'What did your boy-friend say? You were so long he must have told you the whole story of his life—'

'He did, in a way. But now let's order dinner.'

Steak was one of the things she asked for, and stout to wash it down, but I persuaded her to have champagne. 'You'll need it,' I said, 'and so shall I.'

'I don't suppose you could tell me anything that would surprise me.'

'I think I can.' Then suddenly I had a doubt—for what's in a name? Had I jumped to some idiotic conclusion? Was it a damp squib after all?

'I'm waiting,' Doris warned me.

'Well, he's at Restbourne. There, I knew you'd be surprised.'

She recovered herself quickly.

'So are about eighty thousand other people. What's odd in
that?'

'It would take too long to tell you.'

'Everything's taken long tonight.'

'Well, here's your steak at any rate, and my grilled sole.'

I asked the waiter to pour out the champagne. Doris
attacked her steak. 'I'm still waiting,' she said. 'All you've told
me so far is that your friend's at Restbourne. Is that stop-press
news?'

'Well—' I began.

'I wish you wouldn't go on saying "well". What's the use
of a well without any water?'

'It's who he's with.'

'Who *is* he with? A woman, I suppose. Probably a woman
like me. Restbourne is stiff with them.'

I stared at her. I had so often seen the Face coming to life
under Edward's pencil that it had something legendary and
hypnotic about it, something of the immortality of art that
made it more memorable than the living model. If Mona Lisa
had sat beside her portrait, it would have overshadowed her.

'I don't know if she was like you,' I said, 'but she had the
same name, Blackmore.'

That shook her a little, but only for a moment.

'It's a common name—not that we were brought up common. There are loads of Blackmores.'

'Perhaps. But not at the Krazie Café.'

Then I got my effect—the same effect that Edward's announcement had had on me, but more so.

'You don't say so!' she said, and a mist, perhaps the expression of her inner bewilderment, clouded her dark-blue eyes. 'A
Blackmore at the Krazie Café! It doesn't make sense.'

'It didn't to me,' I said.

'I left there five weeks ago—how could I still be there?'

'That's what I asked myself.'

'Sounds dotty, doesn't it?' she said. 'Was he kidding you?'

'He's not that sort of man.'

'What took him to the Krazie Café anyway? What took you, for that matter?'

'Ah, thereby hangs a tale,' I said. 'Some day I'll tell you.' But I didn't think that we should meet again.

'You keep stirring your drink with that long mushroom thing,' she said. 'What good does it do?'

'It takes the effervescence out.'

'You've taken the effervescence out of me. You've knocked me sideways. Well, you're here, and I'm here, so what do we care—'

'You're too young to remember that song.'

'My father used to sing it. "Well", as you're so fond of saying, your friend is at Restbourne with Miss Blackmore—not at the Krazie Café, it shut long ago, and not with me, because I'm here with you. It's amazing, isn't it?'

'It is.'

'You asked him to meet Miss Blackmore in London—I don't know what you meant by it—and he's with another Miss Blackmore at Restbourne. Perhaps he thought we were the same.'

'That's a question for metaphysics.'

'I don't understand your long words. But it is odd. But don't let's let it spoil our evening. . . . He didn't tell you what her other name was?'

'No. But I have just one clue. She must look exactly like you.'

'Like me?'

'Yes, or else he wouldn't be with her.'

Doris frowned, then suddenly her eyebrows lifted and her whole face shone with understanding.

'Why, it's my sister!'

'Your sister?'

'You don't remember much, do you? The twin sister I told you about. The quiet one.'

'I do remember something.'

'I don't keep up with my family much, especially now. I was never any good at writing letters. . . . But it must be her. The sly-boots! She didn't like her job, and always had a hankering for the Krazie. Yes, Gladys, that's who it is. It might almost be me, for she's the dead image of me.'

'The living image.'

'Yes, you're right. She always was a close one. But why should she bother to tell me? I didn't tell her when I went to London. Why write a letter, if you aren't going to get anything out of it? But she's a good girl, if you know what I mean, and I hope he'll be good to her.'

'I'm sure he will.'

'What a chance! It might easily have been me, she's exactly like me, though not so pretty as I am, some people say. Still, good luck to her.'

The full magnitude of her loss was becoming clear to Doris, and the Pêche Melba lay untasted on her plate.

'It may be just a passing fancy for both of them,' I said, but I didn't believe it.

'I wish I was in her shoes. Some people have all the luck.'

Our conversation languished. I thought wonderingly of Edward. What must have been the pressure on his feelings, to take him back to Restbourne, when he had been assured the bird had flown! And his blind faith had been rewarded: I felt sure that as long as Gladys lived, the Face would vanish from his doodlings.

It was getting late. We bandied words for a bit, but there was little zest behind her thrusts and parries. 'If you knew how I felt about you, you wouldn't look so pleased with yourself' was the best she could do.

'It makes you feel old, doesn't it?' she said suddenly.

'What does?'

'Oh, I dunno, the whole thing—seeing your sister get married before you do. You think he'll marry her?'

'I'm sure of it.'

'Jolly good. I never wanted to marry—I've seen too many people part—and I don't expect you do.'

'Well, not at the moment,' I said ungraciously.

She sighed musically.

'Too comfortable, I suppose. Well, I don't blame you. I should like to write to Gladdy, though. We call her Gladdy, or Glad—though she never was glad so as you'd notice. Perhaps she'll be gladder now. I needn't tell her what I'm doing here—she doesn't know, none of them do. But I should like her to know I wish her well. Or do you think I'd better wait until she's hooked him?'

'I think I should.'

'They might not tell me—but he'll tell you, won't he?'

I saw the implication of this, and said rather unwillingly:

'Yes, of course.'

'So if I don't hear, you'll find a way to pass it on. All right? I wonder if they'll invite me to their wedding.'

'I've no doubt they will.'

'The more fools they—I shouldn't, in their place. I suppose it will be ever such a smart wedding—bang on and whizzo. The real McCoy. Heigh ho!' She gave her musical sigh, and looked up at the clock. 'Good lord, I must be off. But I must powder my nose first.'

'Look here,' I said, when she came back, refurbished, 'I've wasted a lot of your time, and it hasn't turned out as I thought it would. If you are disappointed, so am I. Now what about a little remembrance?'

I didn't have to fumble, I had the notes ready in my pocket.

'I've told you before,' she said, rising, 'and I don't mind

telling you again, you've got no respect for a girl's feelings. You can keep your blasted money! I shall tell Uncle Harry I was ill, and so I am—you've made me ill, and I wouldn't go back with you, not even if you asked me!'

She glared at me through unshed tears and for a moment the impression of the Face was so intense that I could hardly see hers for it.

'That's O.K. by me,' I said. 'I don't like these transports so soon after dinner. They give me indigestion.'

At that she laughed, and by the time we reached the pavement—now her haunt—we were friends again. Only a few steps to the kerbstone, but how the tap-tapping of her heels betrayed her! And then a passing taxi bore her off.

The Corner Cupboard

It was the first September of the Second War, and Philip Holroyd had decided to leave his flat in London and settle in the country out of the way of the bombs. The place he hit upon was in the West of England, about four miles from a middle-sized market town which he did not think would interest the enemy. Being a bachelor, and as helpless as bachelors generally are, and also a writer, as helpless as writers generally are, he knew he could not fend for himself: he must have a cook and a daily woman. The house, like many other houses, was called the 'Old Rectory', and was, of course, much too large for Philip; perhaps he would not have taken it but for the urgency of his desire to get away from London. In September 1939 travelling by train was difficult: he paid the house a brief visit, and when he heard that several other people were after it he took it on the nail, being easily influenced by threats. The pride of the well-worn Victorian furniture was a magnificent doll's house, but there were some good pieces of an older date, which, occurring haphazard with the rest, and not given any special prominence, gave the place a kind of dignity and unself-consciousness. These included, in the room Philip had marked out for his bedroom, since among other advantages it had the inestimable one of being nearest to the bathroom, an old mahogany bow-fronted corner cupboard, which, unlike some of the cupboards and chests of drawers, was empty of the owner's possessions. It will do for my medicines, thought Philip, who was something of a hypochondriac.

To find a cook was his most urgent problem. The woman who had looked after him in London, being cockney-born, refused to leave it. He dreaded the thought of having to get used to a new person; he was too timid to give orders with conviction, but at the same time liked things done his way. Having lived for many years alone, he was not at all adaptable and was prone to make mountains out of molehills. Although in London he had plenty of friends his experience with each had become taped: they neither gave nor took from him anything new. The unpredictable was his bugbear. Unconsciously he had withdrawn into himself and grown a shell, albeit a soft one.

Days passed with no news from the Registry Office in Shuttleworth; and when at last they wrote that they had found someone who they thought would suit him it was too late for him to go to interview her; the man in the Foreign Office who had taken his London flat was on the point of moving in. So he engaged Mrs. Weaver without seeing her, but not (as might have happened nowadays) without a reference. 'She is a woman', wrote her late employer, with whom she had stayed a year, 'who needs a good deal of special attention and sympathy which, in our rather large and busy family, she has not always been able to find. She is honest and clean and within her limitations a good cook. Where there is only one in family she would, I think, feel more at home. She responds quickly to encouragement and appreciation. The loss of her husband in the First World War seems to have unsettled her in some ways.'

In her own letter Mrs. Weaver gave her age as forty-six— which happened to be Philip's own age—and said that she hoped to be able to oblige him in every possible way. All this predisposed him in her favour; the need for sympathy and attention was one that, in spite of being an egotist, he was quite ready to meet; indeed, he rather fancied himself as a consoler.

When he arrived at the Old Rectory she was already installed.

For the first day or two, in spite of his resolution to ladle out sympathy and appreciation, he didn't see much of Mrs. Weaver. He was busy trying to assimilate the strangeness of his new surroundings. All those outhouses and stables, which the old rectors had no doubt been able to find a suitable use for; couldn't, indeed, have done without! That weedy court-yard with its central drain, through which the water (it had been raining plentifully) took so long to run away! And the garden with its towering trees, traversed by a sullen but romantic rivulet, how much too large it was for the gardener who was said to come three times a week! And the emptiness and silence, after London! A car coming by (the house faced the village street) was quite an event; one listened to its entire progress, from the first throb of the engine to the last. And soon, if petrol-rationing really became a fact, these irruptions into the silence would be fewer, almost non-existent! Already he could hear his own footsteps, the footsteps of a single man, walking alone. Isolation made Philip Holroyd busy with his thoughts as never before; they had the intensity of sensations. Then suddenly he remembered Mrs. Weaver and her need for sympathy.

'Excuse me,' he said, going into the kitchen. Flanked by a larder and a pantry and a second kitchen, and having a back-stairs defended by a door opening out of it, it was a room where meals for twenty people might have been prepared. 'Excuse me,' he repeated, for he was a man who liked to err on the side of politeness, 'but I wanted to tell you how very much I enjoyed the supper you gave me last night. The cheese soufflé was a dream, and it is such a test of cooking.'

Mrs. Weaver looked up at him from the deal table where she was making pastry. Her hands were floury. Her face was round and pink, framed by soft brown hair that was going grey. She parted it in the middle; it was thin and straggled a little, but not untidily. Her figure was short and compact. She had a pleasant, almost sweet expression, which didn't change much when she spoke.

'I'm glad you liked it,' she said. 'I always say that men are easier to cook for than women.'

'Oh, do you think so?'

'Yes, they have better appetites for one thing. My husband—' She stopped.

'Yes?'

'He had a very good appetite. He was a guardsman, you know—in the Grenadiers. He was a fine big man. You remind me of him, sir.'

Philip was slightly above middle height. A sedentary life had thickened his figure, and doubled his chin, but he couldn't help being pleased at being compared to a guardsman.

'And for all he was so big,' went on Mrs. Weaver, 'he was like a child in some ways. He went on playing with soldiers to the end—he was that proud of his regiment. He hated the Coldstream Guards and wouldn't hear them mentioned. I nursed him all through his last illness, when the hospital threw him out, saying they could do nothing more for him. I washed him and shaved him and did everything for him. If you were to fall ill, sir—'

'Oh, I hope I shan't,' said Philip hastily. 'But it's nice to think—' he didn't finish the sentence. 'By the way,' he said, 'is there anything you want? Anything I can do for you to make you more comfortable? I'm afraid your room isn't very comfortable.'

'Oh, no, sir, I'm very happy with you. But there's just one thing—'

'What is it?' asked Philip, when she hesitated.

'Well, sir, it sounds so silly.'

'Never mind, I'm often silly myself.'

'I hardly like to tell you.'

'Out with it.'

'It's the small tortoiseshell butterfly, sir. I can't bear the sight of it. There was one fluttering about the room when my husband was dying. When I see one I go—'

Philip took a hasty glance round the darkening kitchen.

'I don't know much about the habits of small tortoiseshell butterflies,' he said, 'but I fancy they only breed once a year, in the summer. If you happen to see a stray one, call me and I'll get rid of it. I'm quite handy with a butterfly-net.' He made a mental note to buy one.

'Thank you,' she answered, without smiling. 'And I don't like anything that's made of tortoiseshell, either. It makes me want to . . .'

'I'll see there isn't any,' said Philip firmly. 'I'll go along now and round up every bit I find. There's a cigarette-box in my sitting-room— But I'm afraid you must be lonely, as well as having too much to do. Mrs. Featherstone is coming in tomorrow, the daily woman, you know. She lives in the village. She'll be company for you.'

Mrs. Weaver didn't seem to welcome this idea.

'At any rate she'll only be here in the mornings,' she said.

Philip bowed himself out and made straight for the cigarette-box. It was a useful object and a nice one, with *Cigarettes* scribbled across the lid in silver, and silver mountings at the corners. A wedding-present perhaps. But it must go, and so must the buhl clock on the chimney-piece. How bare the room looked without them! What else? Philip ranged the house for the dark, seductive gleam of tortoiseshell, suddenly developing an attachment for the substance that he had never had before; the sense of so many unoccupied rooms all round him gave him an odd feeling; but his search went unrewarded until he came to his own bedroom where, on the dressing-table, lay his comb. He could easily do without it for a day or two; its job was almost a sinecure, he had so little hair. But where to put the culprits so that they shouldn't offend Mrs. Weaver's vision and make her do—whatever they did make her do? In the corner cupboard, of course. There she would never see them.

He opened the two rounded doors, and stood and stared. Unpacking, he had heaped his pharmacopoeia (almost his first thought was for it) on to the two lower shelves of the corner cupboard. He had never counted the separate items but there must be nearly thirty. He hadn't bothered to set them straight or even to stand all of them up: that was to be for another day, the day until which Philip postponed so many things. And now they were all arranged and tidy.

Philip's first reaction was one of gratitude to Mrs. Weaver, who had taken so much trouble for him. His second was more complex. On the middle shelf the medicines had been put in the way that any tidy-minded person might have put them. But on the lowest shelf they had been arranged in a certain order that betrayed intention and design. They had been *drawn up* in a kind of formation, the tallest bottles lining the cupboard wall, the medium-sized ones in front of them, and at the feet, so to speak, of these, a third row of smaller vessels, jars and tubes and such-like. The two formations faced each other at right angles, and in between was an empty triangular space like a stage, which seemed to be waiting for something to happen.

Clearly it all meant something: but what did it mean?

Then the meaning flashed on Philip. The bottles were soldiers, two sides drawn up for combat: and the space between them was a battlefield.

He smiled at this odd fantasy of Mrs. Weaver's; it was some kind of psychological legacy from her guardsman-husband, who in his last illness used to play at soldiers. And yet mingling with his amusement was a faint uneasiness; there was too much tension, too much implied enmity in the little scene for it to have been set for comedy. Philip was sensitive to the influence of objects; he responded not only to their aesthetic

C

but to their personal appeal. Among the bits and pieces that he had brought from London was a silk Heriz rug. He liked all Eastern carpets but the silk rugs of Heriz had a special fascination for him, particularly this one. Framing a brick-red ground its border had a scrolling pattern in crimson; and the crimson reappeared in figures on the ground itself together with other colours, palest buff and turquoise blue. But it was the wooing of the two reds that most delighted him. In favoured moments he could get an ecstasy from contemplating it that amounted to a minor mystical experience. The best moment was when he was called; then, tea-cup in hand, he would fix his eyes on the rug beside his bed and await ravishment.

Here was another kind of symbolism and Philip didn't altogether like it. . . . But the top shelf was still unoccupied. Into it he put the little clock, the cigarette-box and the comb, all the gleanings of his tortoiseshell harvest. He thrust them to the back, without any regard to military formation, and in front of them erected a barricade of miscellaneous objects—a long roll of cotton-wool in a blue wrapper, some packets of paper handkerchiefs, and other things of vaguely medical use, which effectually obscured them.

Putting the matter out of his mind he was turning to go when a thought struck him: Why not lock the medicine-cupboard? He went back. The cupboard had a lock, and it had a key; but the key didn't turn in the lock, and the tongue of the lock had no slot to fit into—the slot had been torn out. Philip frowned. The vandalism of these days! The deception, so characteristic of them, of fitting a sham lock which didn't do its job! The eyewash! Then he smiled at himself and almost blushed. What had induced him to think of locking the cupboard, as if it was some sort of Bluebeard's chamber, as if it harboured a threat! It was too silly, and might offend Mrs. Weaver, whose only fault was that she had been kind enough to tidy up for him. Besides, she would have no reason to go to the cupboard again; it would be the daily woman's job to 'do' his bedroom; Mrs. Weaver wasn't even under contract to 'do' his sitting-room—the 'lounge' as she called it.

At eight o'clock next day Mrs. Weaver brought him his early morning tea. Bethinking himself, he said, 'How kind of you to put my medicine-cupboard straight. It was in an awful mess.' She gave him a surprised, uncomprehending look, so he repeated what he had said, with additional expressions of gratitude. Still getting no reply he asked her to give him his bed-jacket. This she did, at once, helping him into it with affectionate concern.

Presently he began to hear the whirr of the carpet-sweeper, the swish of dustpan and brush, the creak and thump of moving furniture, noises which sound so sweetly in the ear of the lie-abed. Mrs. Featherstone, of course! He must remember to have a word with her. At last his staff problem was solved: everything was under control.

There remained the orders—the kitchen orders—for the day. At half-past ten Mrs. Weaver came into his sitting-room with a preoccupied air, but without the writing-pad she usually carried. She came to a stand in front of him, her hands clasped across her body. Philip rose.

'I'm afraid I can't stay with you any longer,' she said. 'You see, I've become too fond of you.'

Philip was utterly taken aback. His first impulse was to resent this intrusion on his feelings which he had guarded from assault for so many years. Dismay succeeded resentment as he saw his domestic edifice crumbling.

'You see, I've become too fond of you,' Mrs. Weaver repeated inexorably.

Philip had to say something.

'You'll ... you'll get over that,' he faltered. 'These things ... do happen, but ... they soon wear off. You ... you will find someone else.' Not too soon, I hope, he added mentally.

'I was very fond of my husband,' said Mrs. Weaver, 'but it was nothing to what I feel for you.'

Philip longed to say, 'Oh, don't be silly!' but he was a kind-hearted though a far from passionate man, and felt he must meet her on a human plane. But how? He had never received a declaration of love before.

'Don't you think you could give it a trial?' he coaxed. 'I mean, to stay here and see how you felt in a few days' time? You might see another side of me, you might even'—his voice rose hopefully—'come to dislike me!'

Bursting into tears Mrs. Weaver left the room.

Philip paced up and down it, breathing out noisy sighs. How clumsy he had been! Yet could he have done better? Had she mistaken the expressions of sympathy and appreciation which her previous employer had enjoined on him, for signs of love? Utterly at a loss, half rueful, half angry, he wandered into the passage where he met Mrs. Featherstone, sweeping the stairs. At the sight of him she straightened up; a tallish woman, pain-fully thin, with a high complexion, bleached blue eyes, and frizzy hair dyed almost red. Longing to talk to someone, he engaged her in conversation, and so much did he appreciate her tart and salty remarks, in which no hint of a tender emotion was discernible, that he chattered far more freely, and more intimately, than he meant to, and was only deterred from taking her into his confidence about Mrs. Weaver by noticing that the kitchen door, a short way down the passage, was half-open, like a listening ear.

'Oh,' he broke off, 'you must be wanting your elevenses. See you tomorrow, shan't I?'

Mrs. Weaver did not return to the topic of her affection; she neither withdrew her notice nor renewed it, and Philip began to hope that she was thinking better of it. Try as he would, he couldn't meet her on the old cordial terms; his voice, he knew, was distant and formal, his enunciation too distinct, and his good-night cold. Shutting his bedroom door he vaguely felt he was shutting something out. Perhaps he needed a tranquillizer, a dose of bromide. He went to the corner cupboard.

At first he didn't take in what he saw, he only realized there was a change. The stage which had been empty was now occupied—but by what? At the back a small broken bottle reared its jagged edges, its base strewn with splintered glass; and in front of it lay a white object made of cotton-wool, roughly shaped to form a female figure. But it wasn't white all over, for covering the middle of the body was the blood-red petal of a rose. Beside the prostrate figure, pointing at its vitals, was the unsheathed blade of Philip's pocket-knife.

Otherwise there was no change: the serried ranks of bottles looked on, unmoved in any sense.

Philip backed away, severely shaken. He tried to tell himself that it was all an accident—well, not an accident, his pen-knife couldn't have got there by accident, nor could the cotton-wool, but somebody rummaging in the medicine-cupboard, not meaning anything special, perhaps trying to get a bottle out (some servants didn't think that taking their employer's medicine was stealing), might have produced these odd, surrealist effects. For a moment he thought of calling Mrs. Weaver and confronting her with it; but how did he know she had done it? The daily woman might have.

Somehow he felt he couldn't go to sleep with that thing in the room; it had the air of being dynamic, not static; the intention that created it was still at work. He couldn't lock his bedroom door, it had no key. He would have liked to move into another room; but would the bed be aired? Better the ju-ju concoction in the corner cupboard than a damp bed. But he would need something stronger than bromide now; one of those small red sausages from the phial that seemed to kneel so gloatingly beside the . . . well, the corpse. Overcoming his distaste he gingerly detached the phial from its rank, and opening it swallowed two capsules.

'Good morning, Mrs. Weaver,' he said, as she placed the tray by his bedside. Feeling muzzy, he was slow to come to himself. 'Would you mind giving me my bed-jacket?' When she did not appear to hear, a resentment against her mounted in him, and he said with anger in his voice, 'Would you be good enough to give me my bed-jacket?' Said in that imperious way the request sounded silly, and his resentment mounted. 'Can't you give me that jacket?' he almost shouted, and then she handed it to him, holding it away from her as though it was something that needed decontamination. 'Look here,' he said. 'When I give you an order, I expect you to obey it, do you hear?' She didn't answer, and her silence seemed to give her an advantage over him. 'And there's another thing,' he said. 'Are you responsible for that tomfoolery in the medicine-cupboard?' And when again she didn't answer he jumped out of bed and, taking her roughly by the arm, pushed her towards the cupboard and opened the doors. 'Look at that filthy mess,' he said. 'Did you do it, or didn't you?'

At last she found her tongue. 'I didn't do it,' she said with some dignity. 'I know nothing about it.'

'All right,' fumed Philip, 'I shall ask Mrs. Featherstone to clean it up.'

'Ask her by all means,' Mrs. Weaver said.

After breakfast Philip Holroyd felt bitterly ashamed of his outburst. It was unlike him to lose his temper, and for such a trivial reason, too. He blamed the sleeping-draught, which sometimes made him irritable, and more mortifyingly, a kind of sex-resentment which Mrs. Weaver's declaration of the morning before had kindled in him. Poor woman, she had every right to fall in love with him, preposterous as it seemed;

and had not Goethe said, 'That I should love you is no concern of yours'? When she came in to take the orders he would
apologize to her, but meanwhile a mess was a mess, and he
must ask Mrs. Featherstone to clean out the medicine-
cupboard—ask her guardedly, of course, because in view of
Mrs. Weaver's denial, she might have done it herself; after
all, his bedroom was her province. But he didn't think she had.
What dire offence from amorous causes springs! Unless he
kept watch on his tongue he might lose both his retainers. Perhaps he had better take the blame himself.

Could he have done it himself? Writers were notoriously
absent-minded. The thought was disquieting but it was also
too fantastic, and going to look for Mrs. Featherstone he dismissed it from his mind.

He could not find her, nor could he hear anywhere the in-
definable but unmistakable sounds of her presence. The house
was silent. Returning to his sitting-room he saw, what aston-
ishingly had before escaped his notice, that the room had not
been touched since yesterday. It looked stale, tired, and untidy.
Explanations chased each other across his mind. Cleaning-
women were notoriously fickle. Perhaps Mrs. Featherstone had
taken a dislike to him; perhaps she had interpreted his too
forthcoming manner yesterday as a sign of deeper feeling, just
as Mrs. Weaver had. Perhaps—

Before he went into the kitchen he found himself knocking
at the door. Mrs. Weaver's manner was neutral; she showed
neither pleasure nor displeasure at his entrance. Had she seen
Mrs. Featherstone? No. Had she any idea why Mrs. Featherstone hadn't come? No, she wasn't interested in Mrs. Featherstone's affairs. These daily women—

'Then I had better go and see her,' Philip said. 'Meanwhile,
for lunch I might have—, and for dinner—. The omelette last
night was delicious. What a good cook you are, Mrs. Weaver!'

.   .   .   .   .

How pleasant to be away from the house and in the open air! Philip quite enjoyed his ramble down the broad, straggling village street, liberally besprinkled with cowpats, pleasantly aglow with September sunshine. But when he reached Mrs. Featherstone's white-washed cottage with its porch of trellis-work, her daughter told him she was ill in bed. 'Mum's none too good,' she said. 'The doctor calls it a haemorrhage. All to do with those ulcers. She's always been too thin, he says.'

Walking back, Philip didn't notice the sunshine, or the country sights and sounds. He went straight up to his bedroom and peeped inside the medicine-cupboard. Not seeing very well he opened the doors wide. It had been swept and garnished. Once more the serried ranks of soldier-bottles guarded an empty stage.

So several days went by without more manifestations, and Philip began to put the whole thing at the back of his mind. He was punctual in inquiring about Mrs. Featherstone, however. She had been taken to hospital, and every day her condition was said to be 'unchanged'. Philip's efforts to replace her were unsuccessful. Two women came to see him; he showed them over the house, making light of its size, and introduced them to Mrs. Weaver, who though not affable was not ungracious; but neither wanted the job, and when they went away gave him the impression that they had come out of curiosity.

Without more manifestations . . . But Philip had cheated. He had made a rule not to look inside the corner cupboard unless he really required some medicine. This seemed sensible. What was less sensible was that more than once, when he did need some, for minor ailments brought on by the chalky water, he refrained. Why? Because, he told himself, he had got into the habit of taking too much medicine. The real reason, which he didn't acknowledge, was a reluctance to open the medicine-cupboard door.

Oh, but this fibrositis, which a single application of liniment would charm away! 'Mrs. Weaver!' he called down the passage. 'Have you any oil of wintergreen?'

'What for, sir?'

'To rub on my stiff neck.'

'I'm afraid I haven't, sir.'

'Then would you be an angel and fetch me a bottle out of my medicine-cupboard? A smallish bottle, on the left side, I think.'

Mrs. Weaver, the catspaw!

In she came, bearing the bottle.

'Shall I give your neck a rub, sir?'

'Oh, no, thank you. I can do it quite easily myself.'

'I often used to rub my husband's neck, sir.'

'Did he have fibrositis too?'

'Yes, and not only in his neck, sir. He had it all over him. I could give you a rub, sir.'

'I'm sure you could, but I think I can manage.'

'It's easier for someone else to do it, sir.'

'But it's such a sticky business.'

'Not if you only use the tips of the fingers. I always use my finger-tips. They are much more sensitive.'

'I'll remember to use mine,' Philip said.

'Excuse me, sir, but have you any objection to my rubbing you? It always did my husband so much good.'

Now don't lose your head, Philip told himself, but impatience got the upper hand.

'If you think I'm your husband—'

'I don't, sir, my husband was a guardsman and a gentleman, not an Oxford undergraduate and a cad.'

'I'm sure he was,' said Philip, far too angry to relish being called an undergraduate. 'I'm sure he was, but did he never tell you—'

'Tell me what, sir?'

c*

'Well, to leave him alone?'

Aghast at the cruelty of these words, Philip closed his eyes. When he opened them Mrs. Weaver had gone.

He put off rubbing his stiff neck until he went to bed. To do so suited his habit of procrastination—just another half-hour before I start rubbing! Also it would be more prudent, as well as pleasanter, to get straight into bed after the operation: less likelihood of catching a chill. Also, if he did it on his way to bed one wash and one undressing would take the place of two, for he would have to take some clothes off to get at his neck. And he would not dirty his vest and shirt as well as his pyjamas. But the chief cause of the postponement was a different one. After Mrs. Weaver's exit he had had the usual revulsion of feeling about her. He had behaved abominably to her and he ought to apologize. The best way of apologizing would be to call her in and ask her to rub his neck after all. 'I'm so sorry I was irritable, Mrs. Weaver. Please forget about it, if you can, and give my neck a rub. Just wait a minute while I take my shirt off.' He rehearsed these sentences and others like them, but somehow couldn't bring himself to act upon them. Since the incident he had only seen Mrs. Weaver's face beyond the hatch when she put the food through, and it told him nothing. At what time did she retire for the night? At about half-past nine, he thought, and kept involuntarily looking at the clock, his neck protesting sharply as he did so. But the clock wasn't on the chimney-piece, it was in the corner cupboard, and probably not going, since he had omitted to wind it up. How silly: he had his wrist-watch, of course, and it said ten o'clock. If he called her now she would probably be in bed, and come down in her nightgown or her pyjamas, or whatever slumberwear she favoured, and that would never do.

He felt an unaccountable unwillingness to go to bed, and lingered on watching the dying fire. A fire made work; he oughtn't to have it, really, now that he was without a daily woman: tomorrow he would tell Mrs. Weaver not to light it.

At last he dragged himself upstairs, but when he reached his bedroom he realized he had forgotten the oil of wintergreen. He must turn the lights on and go back and fetch it. Down he went through the quiet house. It was on the sideboard where Mrs. Weaver had left it, and even at a distance exhaled a strong whiff of her presence. Its own smell, when he took the cork out, was much more reassuring.

Remember the finger-tips... He rubbed gently along his neck, and as far round to the back as he could reach; Mrs. Weaver was right: it was easier for someone else to do it, but that someone had to be the right one, which she was not. He lengthened out the process, turning up the bottle, taking little nips, as if he was a wintergreen addict.

Now there was no excuse for these delaying tactics: he must get into bed. But before getting into bed, he must put back the bottle—put it back into the corner cupboard.

But why? Why not leave it on his dressing-table till the morning, when somebody else—Mrs. Weaver in fact—would put it back? He wasn't mad about the corner cupboard and she was, or seemed to be: if he put it back he would deprive her of a pleasure. But he saw through his own cowardice, for cowardice it was; he mustn't let it grow on him, mustn't let neurosis grow on him, or soon he wouldn't be able to do the simplest thing, not cross the street, perhaps, which was far more dangerous, even in the country, than putting a medicine-bottle back into its place.

When he was only a few feet from the cupboard he heard the sound of something dripping. Was it the tap from his wash-basin? But no, the tap was turned off. Back he came and saw, couldn't help seeing, a dark pool like an inky sunburst on the bare boards below the cupboard. He stooped to touch it; his upturned finger came back red, not black.

A quotation, or perhaps a misquotation, from Landor stole into his mind: 'Dost thou hear the blood drip, Dashka?'

The curtains were flung back, the stage appeared: rather the same scene as last time, but there were differences. Another bottle faced him, its neck broken and cracked down all its length. Through the crack the red cough-mixture oozed. The cotton-wool corpse, white dabbled with red, was not a woman's but a man's; elementary as the modelling was, the figure was faintly obscene. And the blade of the pocket-knife, instead of pointing at the vitals of the victim, was plunged into its neck. There was something else too, the explanation of which didn't dawn on Philip at the time: a sliver of coarse yellowish paper, cut out of a telegram: SEVERELY WOUNDED, it said.

Rage struggled with terror in Philip's breast, but for the moment rage prevailed. Magic, indeed! He'd show her! He'd give her magic! But what, and how? His mind had never worked along those lines before. He looked up. On the top shelf lay the fat roll of cotton-wool in its flimsy wrapping of blue paper which he had intended as a barricade against the evil influences of the tortoiseshell. Had Mrs. Weaver, prying in the cupboard, moved it, and had the sight of what lay behind it touched her off? ... She had plucked it like a goose: feathers of cotton-wool were everywhere, mingled with thin shreds of blue paper. Philip followed suit, and soon had fashioned from the yielding medium the grotesque likeness of a female form. But what to do with it? Exactly what harm did he intend her? What kind of death were those implacable soldier-bottles to witness?

The doll's house on the landing just outside his door possessed a kitchen, and the kitchen had a stove, a big old-fashioned thing with an oven-door that opened. He took the stove out and suddenly his evil purpose seemed to animate it, giving it the cold fascination of a lethal instrument. But he must clean the cupboard first, for no blood was to flow. He must shift the scene so that no competing image should weaken its effect. He worked with nailbrush, soap and towel—Mrs. Weaver kept her kitchen very clean. How much verisimilitude should he aim at? He wanted his tableau to be death-like, not life-like. Softly he closed the oven-door on the plump neck; the head was well inside; the arms and legs and trunk sprawled outwards. His horror of himself increased almost to faintness; through the salutary odours of the medicine-cupboard he thought he could detect a whiff of gas. And there must be one, there must be. He turned his bedroom gas-fire on, and listened to the exciting continuous susurration of escaping gas. Death could breathe out without ever breathing in. But *he* could not, and it was to escape himself and his own fate, not to hasten Mrs. Weaver's, that he turned the tap off and lurched out of the room.

In which of the outhouses he spent the night he never knew. But it gave him a sense of security so profound that under it he slept and slept and slept. Only by degrees, as he was crossing the courtyard in the broad daylight, did memory of the night before return to him, and then only as shapes and colours of feeling, not as facts. But by the time he reached his door he had more or less reconstructed the story. It horrified him; the future yawned at his feet.

Hardly had he got into bed and kicked out his cold hot-water bottle when there came a knock at the door and Mrs. Weaver entered, bringing his morning tea. She drew the curtains and, without being asked, handed him his bed-jacket.

'How is your neck this morning, sir?' she inquired.

Philip turned his head. It hurt him very much, which was strange, for he had felt nothing of it for ten hours.

'Not much better, I'm afraid,' he said.

'You should have let me rub it, sir. My husband—'

'Ah, how good you were to him,' said Philip. 'And yet he died in the end, poor fellow.'

She made no answer but sniffed the air and said,

'There's a slight smell of gas in here. Shall I open the window wider?'

'Do.'

'I always think gas is dangerous,' she went on. 'And so I'm afraid I must give in my notice.'

'Oh, Mrs. Weaver!'

'Yes, I must leave today, and I'll forgo my wages. I had a dreadful dream.'

'Oh, what?'

'That I was being gassed. That I had put my head in a gas-oven. What could have made me dream that?'

'What indeed? But dreams go by contraries, you know,' said Philip.

'I'm not so sure,' said Mrs. Weaver, pensively. 'I'm not so sure. I've ordered the taxi for ten o'clock. I will cook your breakfast.'

On an impulse Philip jumped out of bed. His foot struck against something hard—it was a skewer, a meat skewer.

'Mrs. Weaver,' he called after her, 'you've forgotten something.'

When she came back he handed her the skewer.

'A skewer?' she said. 'However did that get here?' It dropped from her fingers and lay between them, pointing, he was glad to see, in her direction. She stooped to pick it up.

'No, leave it,' he said. 'I'll see to it. And there are two things you can do for me.'

'Yes, sir.'

'First, would you telephone to Shuttleworth Hospital and ask how Mrs. Featherstone is?'

She came back with her neutral face, and said that Mrs. Featherstone had taken a turn for the better.

'And now would you kindly put the bottle of wintergreen back into the medicine-cupboard?'

From the bed he watched her open the bow-fronted doors. One glance showed him that all his magic apparatus of the night had been dismantled.

'Tell me one thing,' he said. 'Do you know who tidied up the medicine-cupboard?'

'No, sir,' she said, and closed the door behind her. Fingering the meat skewer, which was long, thin, sharp and crowned by the traditional crook, Philip almost, but not quite, believed her.

Below him on the blue rep carpet, the Heriz rug, which had lain unregarded for the past few days, suddenly caught his eye. At first to his bewildered mind it seemed a rug like any other; then slowly it began to assert itself and declare its wordless message. Who had woven it, he wondered, who had coloured it with his thoughts? What passions had gone into it, at the confluence of the pale red and the dark? He could not tell nor did it matter; indeed nothing seemed to matter when once the silken spell began to work.

The Waits

CHRISTMAS Eve had been for all the Marriners, except Mr. Marriner, a most exhausting day. The head of the house usually got off lightly at the festive season, lightly that is as far as personal effort went. Financially, no; Mr. Marriner knew that financially quite a heavy drain was being made on his resources. And later in the evening when he got out his cheque-book to give his customary presents to his family, his relations and the staff, the drain would be heavier. But he could afford it, he could afford it better this Christmas than at any other Christmas in the history of his steadily increasing fortune. And he didn't have to think, he didn't have to choose; he only had to consult a list and add one or two names, and cross off one or two. There was quite a big item to cross off, quite a big item, though it didn't figure on the list or on the counterfoil of his cheque-book. If he saw fit he would add the sum so saved to his children's cheques. Jeremy and Anne would then think him even more generous than he was, and if his wife made any comment, which she wouldn't, being a tactful woman, he would laugh and call it a Capital Distribution— 'capital in every sense, my dear!'

But this could wait till after dinner.

So of the quartet who sat down to the meal, he was the only one who hadn't spent a laborious day. His wife and Anne had both worked hard decorating the house and making arrangements for the party on Boxing Day. They hadn't spent the time

in getting presents, they hadn't had to. Anne, who was two
years older than Jeremy, inherited her mother's gift for present-
giving and had made her selections weeks ago; she had a sixth
sense for knowing what people wanted. But Jeremy had left
it all to the last moment. His method was the reverse of Anne's
and much less successful; he thought of the present first and the
recipient afterwards. Who would this little box do for? Who
would this other little box do for? Who should be the fortu-
nate possessor of this third little box? In present-giving his
mind followed a one-way track; and this year it was little
boxes. They were expensive and undiscriminating presents and
he was secretly ashamed of them. Now it was too late to do
anything more: but when he thought of the three or four
friends who would remain un-boxed his conscience smote
him.

Silent and self-reproachful, he was the first to hear the singing outside the window.

'Listen, there's some carol-singers!' His voice, which was
breaking, plunged and croaked.

The others all stopped talking and smiles spread over their
faces.

'Quite good, aren't they?'

'The first we've had this year,' said Mrs. Marriner.

'Well, not the first, my dear; they started coming days ago,
but I sent them away and said that waits must wait till Christmas Eve.'

'How many of them are there?'

'Two, I think,' said Jeremy.

'A man and a woman?'

Jeremy got up and drew the curtain. Pierced only by a
single distant street-lamp, the darkness in the garden pressed
against the window-pane.

'I can't quite see,' he said, coming back. 'But I think it's a
man and a boy.'

'A man and a boy?' said Mr. Marriner. 'That's rather unusual.'

'Perhaps they're choristers, Daddy. They do sing awfully well.'

At that moment the front-door bell rang. To preserve the character of the house, which was an old one, they had retained the original brass bell-pull. When it was pulled the whole house seemed to shudder audibly, with a strangely searching sound, as if its heart-strings had been plucked, while the bell itself gave out a high yell that split into a paroxysm of jangling. The Marriners were used to this phenomenon, and smiled when it made strangers jump: tonight it made them jump themselves. They listened for the sound of footsteps crossing the stone flags of the hall, but there was none.

'Mrs. Parfitt doesn't come till washing-up time,' said Mrs. Marriner. 'Who'll go and give them something?'

'I will,' Anne said, jumping up. 'What shall I give them, Daddy?'

'Oh, give them a bob,' said Mr. Marriner, producing the coin from his pocket. However complicated the sum required he always had it.

Anne set off with the light step and glowing face of an eager benefactor; she came back after a minute or two at a much slower pace and looking puzzled and rather frightened. She didn't sit down but stood over her place with her hands on the chair-back.

'He said it wasn't enough,' she said.

'Wasn't enough?' her father repeated. 'Did he really say that?'

Anne nodded.

'Well, I like his cheek.' Even to his family Mr. Marriner's moods were unforeseeable; by some chance the man's impudence had touched a sympathetic chord in him. 'Go back and say that if they sing another carol they shall have another bob.'

But Anne didn't move.

'If you don't mind, Daddy, I'd rather not.'

They all three raised questioning faces to hers.

'You'd rather not? Why?'

'I didn't like his manner.'

'Whose, the man's?'

'Yes. The boy—you were right, Jeremy, it is a boy, quite a small boy—didn't say anything.'

'What was wrong with the man's manner?' Mr. Marriner, still genial, asked.

'Oh, I don't know!' Anne began to breathe quickly and her fingers tightened on the chair-back. 'And it wasn't only his manner.'

'Henry, I shouldn't—' began Mrs. Marriner warningly, when suddenly Jeremy jumped up. He saw the chance to redeem himself in his own eyes from his ineffectiveness over the Christmas shopping—from the general ineffectiveness that he was conscious of whenever he compared himself with Anne.

'Here's the shilling,' Anne said, holding it out. 'He wouldn't take it.'

'This will make it two,' their father said, suiting the action to the word. 'But only if they sing again, mind you.'

While Jeremy was away, they all fell silent, Anne still trying to compose her features, Mr. Marriner tapping on the table, his wife studying her rings. At last she said:

'They're all so class-conscious nowadays.'

'It wasn't that,' said Anne.

'What was it?'

Before she had time to answer—if she would have answered —the door opened and Jeremy came in, flushed and excited but also triumphant, with the triumph he had won over himself. He didn't go to his place but stood away from the table looking at his father.

'He wouldn't take it,' he said. 'He said it wasn't enough. He said you would know why.'

'I should know why?' Mr. Marriner's frown was an effort to remember something. 'What sort of a man is he, Jeremy?'

'Tall and thin, with a pulled-in face.'

'And the boy?'

'He looked about seven. He was crying.'

'Is it anyone you know, Henry?' asked his wife.

'I was trying to think. Yes, no, well, yes, I might have known him.' Mr. Marriner's agitation was now visible to them all, and even more felt than seen. 'What did you say, Jeremy?'

Jeremy's breast swelled.

'I told him to go away.'

'And has he gone?'

As though in answer the bell pealed again.

'I'll go this time,' said Mrs. Marriner. 'Perhaps I can do something for the child.'

And she was gone before her husband's outstretched arm could stop her.

Again the trio sat in silence, the children less concerned with themselves than with the gleam that kept coming and going in their father's eyes like a dipping headlight.

Mrs. Marriner came back much more self-possessed than either of her children had.

'I don't think he means any harm,' she said, 'he's a little cracked, that's all. We'd better humour him. He said he wanted to see you, Henry, but I told him you were out. He said that what we offered wasn't enough and that he wanted what you gave him last year, whatever that means. So I suggest we give him something that isn't money. Perhaps you could spare him one of your boxes, Jeremy. A Christmas box is quite a good idea.'

'He won't take it,' said Anne, before Jeremy could speak.

'Why not?'

'Because he can't,' said Anne.

'Can't? What do you mean?' Anne shook her head. Her mother didn't press her.

'Well, you are a funny girl,' she said. 'Anyhow, we can but try. Oh, and he said they'd sing us one more carol.'

They set themelves to listen, and in a moment the strains of 'God rest you merry, gentlemen' began.

Jeremy got up from the table.

'I don't believe they're singing the words right,' he said. He went to the window and opened it, letting in a puff of icy air.

'Oh, do shut it!'

'Just a moment. I want to make sure.'

They all listened, and this is what they heard:

> 'God blast the master of this house,
> Likewise the mistress too,
> And all the little children
> That round the table go.'

Jeremy shut the window. 'Did you hear?' he croaked.

'I thought I did,' said Mrs. Marriner. 'But it might have been "bless", the words sound so much alike. Henry, dear, don't look so serious.'

The door-bell rang for the third time. Before the jangling died down, Mr. Marriner rose shakily.

'No, no, Henry,' said his wife. 'Don't go, it'll only encourage them. Besides, I said you were out.' He looked at her doubtfully, and the bell rang again, louder than before. 'They'll soon get tired of it,' she said, 'if no one comes. Henry, I beg you not to go.' And when he still stared at her with groping eyes, she added:

'You can't remember how much you gave him last year?' Her husband made an impatient gesture with his hand.

'But if you go take one of Jeremy's boxes.'

'It isn't a box they want,' he said, 'it's a bullet.'

He went to the sideboard and brought out a pistol. It was

an old-fashioned saloon pistol, a relic from the days when
Henry's father, in common with others of his generation, had
practised pistol-shooting, and it had lain at the back of a
drawer in the sideboard longer than any of them could
remember.

'No, Henry, no! You mustn't get excited! And think of the
child!'

She was on her feet now; they all were.

'Stay where you are!' he snarled.

'Anne! Jeremy! Tell him not to! Try to stop him.' But his
children could not in a moment shake off the obedience of a
lifetime, and helplessly they watched him go.

'But it isn't any good, it isn't any good!' Anne kept repeating.

'What isn't any good, darling?'

'The pistol. You see, I've seen through him!'

'How do you mean, seen through him? Do you mean he's
an impostor?'

'No, no. I've really seen through him,' Anne's voice sank to
a whisper. 'I saw the street lamp shining through a hole in his
head.'

'Darling, darling!'

'Yes, and the boy, too—'

'Will you be quiet, Anne?' cried Jeremy from behind the
window curtain. 'Will you be quiet? They're saying something. Now Daddy's pointing the gun at him—he's got him
covered! His finger's on the trigger, he's going to shoot! No,
he isn't. The man's come nearer—he's come right up to
Daddy! Now he's showing him something, something on his
forehead—oh, if I had a torch—and Daddy's dropped it, he's
dropped the gun!'

As he spoke they heard the clatter; it was like the sound that
gives confirmation to a wireless commentator's words. Jeremy's
voice broke out again:

'He's going off with them—he's going off with them! They're leading him away!'

Before she or any of them could reach the door, Mrs. Marriner had fainted.

The police didn't take long to come. On the grass near the garden gate they found the body. There were signs of a struggle—a slither, like a skid-mark, on the gravel, heel-marks dug deep into the turf. Later it was learnt that Mr. Marriner had died of coronary thrombosis. Of his assailants not a trace was found. But the motive couldn't have been robbery, for all the money he had had in his pockets, and all the notes out of his wallet (a large sum), were scattered around him, as if he had made a last attempt to buy his captors off, but couldn't give them enough.

The Pampas Clump

'BUT what is it you don't like about the pampas clump?' I asked.

'Well, it's untidy for one thing,' Thomas said. 'It doesn't grow evenly and always seems to need a haircut. A shrub should be symmetrical.'

'It isn't exactly a shrub.'

'No, it isn't. A shrub would be more self-controlled. It's a sort of grass—and grass needs cutting. Besides, it's all ages at once, some of it's green, some sere, and some dead. And then its leaves break and dangle depressingly.'

'But aren't we all like that?'

'Not so obviously. We are more of a piece. Anyone would know that you were forty-one, Fergus, and I was thirty-eight.'

I flattered myself that I looked younger than Thomas; there was a deep line between his brows and his eyes behind his spectacles were tired and restless.

'How old is the pampas?'

'Oh, any age. It was here, you may remember, when I bought the house. I've often thought of getting rid of it. It's so suburban. It doesn't fit into an old garden, like this one is supposed to be.'

'But if it's old itself?'

'It must be, or it wouldn't have grown to such a size. But that doesn't make it any the less suburban. People live to a

great age in surburbia, and sometimes grow to a great size....
And besides being untidy, it makes the grass round it untidy
too, it sheds itself.'

'A plant has to live according to its habit,' I argued.

'Yes, but I don't like its habit, or its habits. It offends my
sense of fitness. Besides, it's dangerous.'

'Dangerous?'

'Yes. It looks fragile and wispy, but its leaves are like razors,
they cut you to the bone. It's treacherous and dishonest.'

'Oh, do you think of it as a person?'

Thomas fidgeted.

'No, of course not, except in so far as something you don't
like takes on a personality for you.'

'What sort of personality has it?'

'A semi-transparent one. It blocks the view from the french
window, but if you look hard you can see through it—or you
think you can. I'm always wondering if there isn't someone the
other side of it who can see me though I can't see him or her.'

'Oh, Thomas, how fanciful you are!'

'Well, you try.'

Obediently I screwed my eyes up. The library had two
windows, and from the french window, the one nearest to the
fireplace, by which we were sitting, the pampas clump did
indeed block the view. It cut the line of the hills across the
valley. In the early October twilight it looked quite enormous;
its cone-shaped plumes, stirred by a gentle breeze, swept the
dusky sky, soaring above its downward-curving foliage as a
many-jetted fountain soars above the water fanning outwards
from its basin. And like a fountain, it was, as Thomas had said,
half-transparent. You thought you could see what was behind
it, but you couldn't be sure. That didn't worry me; I rather
liked the idea of the mystery, the *terra incognita* behind the
pampas. And Thomas should have liked it, too. No one ever
called him Tom: at Oxford he was nicknamed Didymus, he

was so much in doubt. Did he dislike the pampas because, in some way, it reminded him of himself, and his own weaknesses? I strained my eyes again, trying to see what lay beyond the soaring feathers and the looped, drooping, reed-like leaves. Perhaps... Perhaps... What did Thomas *want* me to say?

'There *could* be somebody,' I ventured.

'That's what I mean.'

'But he... she... they couldn't see you because...'

'Because why?'

'Because when a shrub.... or something of that sort is near to you, it's more opaque than when it's at a distance. But if you don't like it, why don't you burn it?'

Thomas shuffled in his chair, and answered irritably, 'I don't like destroying things. Besides, it would only rise from its ashes like the phoenix.'

'But if it annoys you—'

'It doesn't annoy me all that much. Besides...' he stopped.

'Besides what?' I prompted.

'You'll think me silly if I tell you.'

'I find all your objections to the pampas frivolous,' I said, 'but tell me.'

'Well, I have a sneaking wish to find out if there *is* someone on the other side of it.'

I didn't laugh because I realized that what he had said meant something to him, something that had been in his mind for a long time. Was it an obsession that he wanted to get rid of, or was he really clinging to it? A ghost that worried him, but one he didn't want to lay? I had an idea.

'When the others come—'

He glanced up. It was half-past six by the French clock on the chimney-piece.

'Are you getting bored?' he asked. 'Julia and Hilary will be here any time now.'

'I didn't mean that,' I said. 'I'm glad to have this chance of talking to you alone. It's so long...I meant, couldn't we arrange a sort of *test*?'

'Of what?'

'Well, of whether there *is* someone behind the pampas clump or not.'

He seemed to ponder deeply. 'I don't know...I don't know. What had you in mind?'

'A sort of procession.'

'A procession? What sort of procession?'

'I hadn't worked out the details.'

Thomas shook his head, fretfully.

'I don't like the idea of a procession. Too many people, and it straggles.'

'Oh, this would be a small, select one.'

'I don't know what you mean,' said Thomas. 'I'm not with you.' There was a sound outside the house, scrunchings and small earth-tremors, and then a silence that indicated arrival. 'Here they are!' said Thomas, getting up and making for the door. 'Guests never seem to arrive at exactly the right time.'

'Have I your permission?—' I called out after him, but I don't think he heard.

Julia I knew quite well; she was fair and round and buxom and in her middle thirties. She had lost her husband in the war; and curiously enough as a widow she was twice the person she had been as a wife. As a wife she had taken on her husband's personality; as a widow she had recovered her own without losing his. Protectiveness was her strong point, and it was clear she had now extended it to Hilary. While her husband was alive she said 'we' more often than she said 'I': she said 'we' still, meaning herself and Hilary.

Hilary I new much less well. She was tall and dark and slender and could look beautiful, but her beauty was ambiguous like the rest of her. I could not make her out, and the more I saw of her the less I understood her. A sphinx without a secret, perhaps. But a sphinx that has, I thought, its attractions for Thomas, for he tried on her many kinds of conversational approach, which she either evaded or answered in a way that he didn't quite expect.

'Are you going abroad, Hilary?'

'Well, as a matter of fact I've just been.'

'Of course, I knew that. You wrote to me from Venice.'

'Did I? I wrote so many letters.'

'We were always writing letters,' Julia put in 'when we weren't sightseeing. Hilary writes such good letters.'

'Do I? I often think they're all about myself, or nothing.'

'Yourself or nothing? Perhaps they are the same,' said Thomas with so much feeling in his voice that it cancelled out the rudeness. 'It's yourself we want to know about. But perhaps you have several selves. Julia's Hilary may be different from mine, and Fergus's different again.'

He raised an eyebrow at me. I thought he carried his probings further than politeness warranted. She didn't seem to resent them but they embarrassed her; she said the word 'I' non-committally and without conviction as if she was not quite sure to what it referred. I didn't want to be drawn but I had to say something—if possible something that would smooth the path for Thomas, who was so obviously taken by her.

'Walt Whitman said you ought to "publish yourself of a personality," ' I remarked.

'That I ought to?'

We laughed.

'No, that everyone ought to.'

Hilary looked troubled.

'That's what I find so difficult!'

'It's one of our problems,' Julia said, smiling, though it was certainly not a problem for her.

'But *are* you going abroad in the winter?' Thomas persisted.

'What do you think, Julia?'

Thomas shook his head in mock despair and before Julia could answer burst out, 'There you go again! Or rather, you don't go—and when you stay—' He spread his hands out, as though to indicate how inconclusive her staying was.

'We will go now,' said Julia huffily, 'and leave you to your port.'

She rose and we rose with her. Hilary was nearly as tall as Thomas; her full, flared skirt swung as she moved. Her charm showed in her movements; they told one something about her that her tongue could not tell.

'Now I like that dress of yours,' said Thomas, 'I like those thin Regency stripes, they are so definite—and the neat rows of forget-me-nots in between. As if we could forget you! It's almost a crinoline, isn't it? Who can tell where it ends and you begin?'

She coloured, and I said to cover her confusion, 'She's like the pampas clump.'

That was how we got back to it again.

It was too dark to do anything now, we decided; tomorrow between tea and dinner, Thomas said, should be the time for our experiment.

'But why so late?' I asked. 'Wouldn't it be better in the full sunlight?'

'How do you mean, better?'

'Well, a better test. In the twilight you might think you were seeing things.'

'We want to see things, don't we?'

'I thought you wanted to make sure, Didymus, that there was nothing . . . or something. As soon as the light begins to go—'

'Doesn't it seem more sporting,' he interrupted, 'to give the mystery a chance? I don't know how I should feel, after all this time, faced by complete certitude.'

'But I thought you wanted it,' I repeated, 'both as regards the pampas clump and . . . and . . .'

'And Hilary? Yes, I suppose I do. I want to be sure about her. But shall I be—about either of them—after the experiment? You called me fanciful, a moment ago.'

'Whatever happens,' I pronounced, 'or doesn't happen, it will change the direction of your thoughts. You won't be able to feel quite the same about . . . either of them again.'

We began to discuss the ways and means, and then Thomas said, 'I think it's time we joined the girls.'

Sunday dragged unbearably: I have seldom been so conscious of the passage of time. The house was liberally provided with clocks, most of them the French Empire type—ladies reclining, children holding baskets of fruits and flowers, all leading a timeless, leisured life. There was hardly one I didn't consult, but the clock in my bedroom was my favourite, because it lagged behind the others and gave me a respite. From what? I didn't really think that anything would come of the experiment, but its increasing nearness provoked a sense of crisis. Ridiculous! It couldn't fail to be a flop—although how much of a flop only Thomas and I should know—for we were not going to take the girls into our confidence—or, of course, the pampas clump itself. More than once during the morning, before Julia and Hilary had made their appearance, and while Thomas was still in church, I went out and studied it. It was a great big thing, the size of a small haystack; it dwarfed the lawn, which was large enough in all conscience, as if it had been a round of beef on a dessert-plate. Like other oversize objects it excited in me, at any rate, mixed feelings of wonder and resentment. Denser in some places than in others, it looked densest when I took my stand outside the french window in the library. Which, for the success of the experiment, ought it to be, transparent or opaque? If transparent, how easy it would be to cheat a little, force one's way into its reedy heart with a pair of secateurs, and thin it out! No one would be the wiser. But wouldn't they? Might not someone see me from a window? Besides, those leaves like razor-blades! I should come back criss-crossed with scratches, or perhaps cut to the bone and pouring blood! 'Why, Fergus, what on earth have you been doing to get into that state?' 'Well, Thomas, I tripped and took a header into the pampas clump, and it savaged me, just as you said it would.'

Giving the plant a wide berth I circled round it, feeling I was being watched. If only I could divide myself in two: become the subject and the object, as one can in thought, then I could make my *alter ego* face me across the pampas. How exciting to see, if I did see him, another Fergus, not a reflection but a real one, perhaps more real than I was! The essential me, in visible form! I had almost transferred Thomas's problem to myself when I looked up and there he was, only a few feet away from me. I had been too much preoccupied to see or hear him coming.

'Spying out the land?' he asked.

I started.

'Yes, I suppose I was.'

He said carelessly:

'You know, I've been thinking it over, perhaps in the light of the Christian faith, which you don't seem to hold—'

'I ought to have gone to church with you, I know.'

'Don't mention it. What I wanted to say was, perhaps we are not meant to see more clearly than we do—through a pampas clump darkly, and all that, and we'd better drop this scheme of ours. What do you think, Fergus?'

'I should be disappointed. What harm can it do? We should just pass by—'

'Oh, it's the principle of the thing. The idea is all right—quite poetical. But if you tried to *live* poetry—'

'Yes?'

'Well, you might come a cropper.... Hullo, here are the girls.'

Hilary was walking a little behind Julia, but Thomas addressed himself to her. 'Good morning, good morning, but it isn't morning, it's afternoon. What have you been doing with yourselves all this time? What have you been doing, Hilary?'

'Nothing much.'

'Nothing much? Couldn't you elaborate that a little?'

'We wrote some letters,' Julia said.

'You're always writing letters, Hilary! Always on paper, never in the flesh! Did you say you were staying here?'

'I used your writing-paper.'

Thomas tried a more direct approach.

'Did you say what fun you were having?'

'I said how nice it was, of course.'

'Did you say anything nice about me?'

Hilary reddened and said with difficulty, 'What else could I say?'

Thomas had to be content with that.

As the dead-line drew near, my heart began to beat uncomfortably. Between six o'clock and dinner is always an awkward time: tea is a thing of the past, drinks are still some way off. Remembering my cue I said:

'What shall we do now?'

To my astonishment Thomas answered, 'Isn't it rather nice sitting here?'

Was he really going to rat on me?

'Very nice,' I said, 'but oughtn't we to do something—something for Hilary to write home about?'

'We've written home,' said Julia, and Hilary stretched her hands towards the newly lit fire.

'You see,' said Thomas, 'she wants to sit among the cinders, warming her pretty little toes, and I should like to sit with her.'

'I have another plan for her,' I said.

'Drop it, Fergus. Forget it.'

I trained an Ancient Mariner's eye on him.

'All day,' I said, 'you've been asking Hilary questions which, if I'm not mistaken, she hasn't always wanted to answer.' I paused to let this sink in. Thomas's face remained expressionless, Julia nodded in approval, Hilary looked as if she wished I hadn't spoken. 'If I carry out my plan,' I went on, with all the impressiveness I could muster, 'Hilary may feel more inclined to answer questions, or Thomas less inclined to ask them.'

'What do you propose, then?' asked Thomas, disingenuously, for he well knew.

I saw that he was weakening.

'Just to go for a walk.'

'Go by all means,' said Thomas, 'but I shan't go with you. I shall stay behind and write letters, like Hilary. Remember, I went to church.'

'If we go for a walk we must change our shoes,' said Julia.

'Need you change yours, Hilary?' Thomas teased her.

She gave him a half-pleading look and got up to go.

'Let's meet in the hall,' I said. 'Mind, no shirking.'

The evening was warm with a slight mist rising from the grass.

'Which way?' asked Julia.

'Round by the silo. I'll show you. I'll go first.' I spoke with authority, as one who leads an expedition.

Julia automatically fell in behind me, and Hilary as auto-

D

matically brought up the rear, and we were moving off when Hilary said, suddenly,

'Need we walk in single file?'

'Only for a minute, until we get our bearings,' and I headed for the far side of the pampas clump, the side away from the house. Reaching it I slowed down, and the little procession, like a cortège, well spaced out, trailed past the clump at a snail's pace.

We went on in this formation for a minute or two: and then Hilary called out: 'Can't we join up now? It's lonely being the cow's tail.'

'Of course,' I said, and stopped. As we were regrouping ourselves, Julia said to Hilary, 'Why, darling, we're looking quite pale—I mean you are. Is anything the matter?'

'I'm all right now,' said Hilary, breathing rather fast. 'Just for a moment something seemed to come over me—a sort of goose-flesh—you seemed so far away, I couldn't reach you! I'm all right now,' she repeated.

'A touch of agoraphobia, perhaps,' I said. 'Let's go arm in arm.' I linked their arms in mine, and so we proceeded until our stumbles brought to an end this always risky method of progression.

'There's the silo,' I told them, as we disengaged ourselves.

'What a horrible object!' cried Julia. 'Why did you choose it for our *but du promenade*?'

'It looks prettier as you get nearer.'

'Oh, nonsense! You must be a surrealist.'

'What do you think, Hilary?' For even I felt impelled to try to drag an opinion out of her.

She answered with unexpected vehemence:

'I hate it—it looks so sinister—it's so black and thick and frightening.'

'Why, it's only a granary!'

'I know that, but let's go another way!'

I suggested the village. 'But,' I warned them, 'we shall lose altitude, we shall have to *climb* back.'

'Oh, Fergus,' cried Julia, 'what a slave-driver you are! Isn't he, Hilary?'

She didn't answer. I pleaded the need of exercise, for me and them; but I didn't explain, as we tramped through the village, and beyond it, that I felt an unaccountable reluctance to go back to the house. What effect would the experiment have had on Thomas? None, I felt sure, but even a negative result would be disappointing. So nearly an hour had passed, and it was growing dark, when weary and footsore (as Julia complained that she and Hilary were) we trudged up the slope to Hill House.

'What's that?'

We were approaching the house from the village, not the garden, side and there was a sort of glare behind it, that outlined the steep roof against the sky and couldn't have been an effect of the sunset, for it waxed and waned.

'What's that?' repeated Julia. 'Is the house on fire?'

'Or a chimney?' said Hilary, for once offering a suggestion. 'The sparks might be —' she stopped.

Sparks there certainly were, but they didn't come out of a chimney-pot; they were being whirled about the sky like fire-flies.

'Take your time,' I said. 'I'll hurry on.'

The pungent smell of burning met me in the hall. 'Thomas!' I called, 'Thomas!' and getting no answer went straight into the library. Here the smell was stronger and the glare fiercer; it lit up the room, lit it up so brightly that I saw at once on the round leather-covered table an envelope with my name scrawled on it. I tore it open.

'Dear Fergus,' I read,

'I saw two figures quite distinctly, yours and Julia's, but not a third, and I'm driven to think that Hilary doesn't exist—at least for me. I only exist for her—so why go on? I don't blame you for wanting me to make sure—I am sure now. You'll find me like Polly Flinders.

Love, Thomas.'

I ran to the window, where the glare came from, but it was not so much the glare that filled my eyes as the huge gap, black and ominous, like a cauldron hung over a furnace, where the pampas clump had been. Beneath it the flames still ran and leapt and spurted on their glowing bed of ashes. Outside the french window I felt their scorching breath upon my face and was soon beaten back. It was not until later, a good deal later, that I and one or two others found the charred remains and near by the twisted shard of the burst pistol which was still too hot to touch.

Won by a Fall

'HAVE you ever tried to live a story?' I once asked a friend of mine. I hadn't seen him for a good many years, and in the meanwhile he had made his name as a novelist.

'Well,' said he, 'I try to live my stories while I'm writing them.'

'I didn't quite mean that. I meant, have you ever read or been told a story which took your fancy so much that you tried to translate it into real life, your own life?'

'You mean a sort of day-dreaming?'

'No, something more definite. I mean a deliberate attempt to make certain events which you've heard about come true, and happen to yourself.'

He thought for a bit.

'I can't say that I have,' he said. 'But if *you* have, tell me. There might be something in it for me.'

After this slender encouragement I began.

'Well, this is the story. It was told me by someone who had read it—I didn't read it myself. There was a man, a big, strong fellow—'

'Like you,' my friend said.

'Yes, to some extent. I couldn't have put myself in his shoes —identified myself with him, or whatever you call it—if he hadn't been. And he was about my age—I was twenty-eight at the time—'

'How long ago was it?'

'About six years. Like me, he was an athlete in a sort of way, and we had other things in common. I worked for a firm in the City, as I daresay you remember—'

'Yes, I think I do.'

'And they used to let me off for Rugger matches, even in the middle of the week. I think they felt I gave them some prestige—though God knows how. The fellow in the story was a policeman—'

'You look rather like a policeman,' said my friend.

'Yes, I've been told so. He went in for wrestling, and sometimes he was excused duty, to take part in a scrap on the mat. Well, this policeman was in love with a girl, but she didn't care for him—I mean she quite liked him, but she was in love with another fellow, a violinist in an orchestra he was, with spectacles and hair falling over his eyes—not the sort of man you'd think a girl would take to.'

I regretted having said this, for my friend was no oil-painting. He was undersized and he wore spectacles. But he was so well known in his own walk of life that I didn't think his appearance mattered to him.

'Did the policeman and the violinist ever meet?' he asked me.

'No, but she used to tell the policeman about him when she was explaining why she couldn't marry him.'

'Oh, they were on those terms?'

'They walked out together quite a lot. She explained that she felt protective towards the violinist, which she couldn't to-wards a policeman, and this policeman was a particularly protective type, besides being a grappler.'

'And you?' my friend said.

'I was courting too, and the girl had a boy-friend, but she was different—she was cagey about him and never let on who he was. But she did say she felt protective towards him. "It's a man's job to protect a woman," I used to tell her, but she couldn't see it that way. In the end I got thoroughly fed up.'

'You're telling your own story now.'

'Only to show the similarities and the differences. I was on a spot just like the policeman was. His mat-work suffered, he lost his appetite, and when he was on the beat he started imagining things—a man with a sack on his shoulder who went into a cul-de-sac (no pun intended) and disappeared—I can't remember the details. And something about seeing an old illuminated manuscript in an ash-can, and when he went back for it, it wasn't there. He thought he was going potty, and all because of this girl.'

'What was she like?' my friend asked.

'I think she was slight and dark and not specially pretty, but she had it for him. Well, one morning about nine o'clock he was strolling along some London street in a dazed sort of way, not having slept—they didn't use sleeping-pills so much in those days—and he slipped on a piece of banana-skin and fell down and couldn't get up. Of course he knew about First Aid and those things, and he knew that something must be wrong. So he just lay there. As it happened there weren't many people about, but presently a girl came up to him, and it was—'

'You needn't tell me,' my friend said. 'It was the girl he was in love with. Talk of coincidences!'

'But they happen, don't they? And many people's lives turn on them. Well, she saw him lying there, looking very pale, with his helmet in the gutter and his leg twisted under him, and in spite of that she recognized him and called for help, and they got him into an ambulance and took him to hospital, and it turned out that his knee-cap was fractured, pretty badly. The surgeon made a mess of setting it, so in the end not only did he have to give up wrestling, he had to leave the police and get a job as a doorman. But—'

'The girl married him,' my friend said.

'How did you guess? She was sorry for him, you see. She thought she could give him something that he needed.'

'And they lived happily ever after?'

'No, not quite. He took to drink, as doormen often do; they work such long hours, they often drop in for a quick one—and the glow of self-sacrifice got a bit dim and sometimes she wished she hadn't made it. That's life, of course.'

My friend agreed. 'But where do you come in?'

'Well,' I said, and somehow it wasn't easy to go on. 'I kept thinking about the story and the more I thought about it the more I got into the policeman's state of mind—half-desperate, you know. I hadn't minded so much before I heard it. I had other girls in my life but the policeman's story seemed to pin-point this one.'

'What was her name?'

'Rosemary.'

My friend made no comment, and I went on, 'Then it occurred to me, Why don't I do what the policeman did? And then I laughed because of what you were saying, was it likely I should slip on a banana-skin just as Rosemary happened to pass by? The chances were too much against it. All the same, the thought kept nagging me, and one evening when she told me she had almost made up her mind to marry this chap—whoever he was—are you married, by the way?'

'No,' my friend said.

'Take my advice, and don't be. Well, that piece of news jolted my imagination and gave me an idea. Why shouldn't I stage an accident like the policeman's? Not a serious one like his, of course, though I should make it look so—I should hobble away, leaning on her arm—and not just anywhere, I wasn't too far gone to see how silly that would be. But I knew of course where Rosemary worked—she was secretary to some sort of executive in a street off Knightsbridge. I used to wonder if he was the man, typists so often fall for their employers. And

I knew what time she had to clock in by—nine-thirty in the morning. We used to save up things to tell each other—I more than her. I had learned her daily schedule by heart—or all of it that mattered to me—so that whenever I thought about her, I should know what she was doing, at any given time. She took the bus along Knightsbridge and then walked down this side-street.'

'And you relied on finding a convenient banana-skin?'

'Ah, there I was clever. But to go back. I worked, as I told you, in the City, practically the same hours as she did, and the City is a long way from Knightsbridge. How could I be there when she was? One afternoon I told my boss I wasn't feeling well and could I have tomorrow off? I'd never gone sick before. I remember his reply, he said: "Yes, of course, Parminter. We've got to keep you fit, haven't we, for the match on Saturday." So the next morning I was there in Wilton Place, walking up and down and—'

'Looking for a banana-skin?' my friend asked.

'No! Even in those days manners had changed, as you must have noticed, and street manners especially. I was *eating* a banana. Between bites I looked up and at last I saw her hurrying along, a little late, towards me. I dropped the banana-skin on the pavement, I put my foot on it, and down I went.'

'Poor Parminter!'

'Well, yes, you're right. I was heavy then—I'm a good deal heavier now—and I came a terrific cropper. My head hit the pavement and I didn't know where I was for a moment. Then I saw Rosemary bending over me.

'"Good God!" she said. "It's Gerald! Are you hurt?"'

I moaned, and tried to stir but couldn't.

'"Darling," she said—it was the first time she had ever called me "darling"—"I know I mustn't try to move you, but I can kiss you," and she did. Then she said, "I'll get an ambulance." I was still feeling groggy when the ambulance drove

D*

up, and it's a blur what happened next, but they let her go with me. At the hospital they X-rayed me, in case I had broken any bones or cracked my skull (you may think it was cracked already!). I hadn't, but they said they must detain me for the night for observation and I was put into a ward with several other cases—orthopaedic, it was called. Rosemary said she would go back to my flat and fetch the things I needed for the night. "Pyjamas? Toothbrush? Toothpaste? Hair-brush? Sponge? Razor? Shaving-brush? Shaving-cream? Bedroom-slippers, dressing-gown?" I had no idea she knew so much about a man's requirements and it all sounded so intimate, as if I'd spent the night with her, which of course I never had— she was too keen on the other fellow. She was back within an hour, but they wouldn't let her see me, because by that time I was suffering from shock—uncontrollable shivers was the form it took. They gave me strong sweet tea and put hot-water bottles round me, I remember. Oh, what a fool I felt, and frightened too: I thought I might have injured myself for life. And what was so mortifying, I had had scores of tumbles playing football, and thought I had learned how to fall. After a time the shivering wore off and then they told me that during the lunch-hour the young lady had telephoned about me twice; she sounded upset, the nurse said, but very sweet. Then a bunch of roses was brought in—roses in February, think of the expense! I took them with me when I left next morning—my bed was needed for another patient. But I could still hardly move: I had a bruise right from my ankle to my hip, and had to be helped into the ambulance and upstairs to my flat. I couldn't get about for several days, and might have starved if Rosemary hadn't come to my rescue. Of course, I missed the match.'

'But not the other match?' my friend said.

'Oh no, I married her.' While I was trying to think what to say next, he said:

'But wasn't that what you wanted?'

'Yes, but it didn't last.'

'Why not?'

'I'll tell you. One day—it was the third anniversary of our wedding day—we had a celebration. It was a slap-up affair, for I'd been doing well, and when we got home, I, being a bit tiddly told her the whole story, how I had faked the fall, and all that. I thought it would amuse her, but it didn't. She burst into tears and said, "You deceived me—I need never have married you." I was as upset as she was. I tried to make her understand that what I did, I did for love of her. But she wouldn't listen. She kept saying I had played a trick on her emotions. "You didn't need me, you only wanted me. You've never had anything the matter with you from that day to this! You're the most self-sufficient man I know—you always fall on your feet!"

' "Well, I didn't that time",' I couldn't help saying.

' "Nor this time either," she sobbed, angrier than ever, and the next morning she left me.'

I couldn't have said those words so calmly once; but it was three years ago.

My friend got up and walked about the room.

'And so you lived the story,' he said, 'or part of it.'

'There isn't any more,' I said. 'She went off with another man—the man she'd always been fond of, I suspect—and asked me to divorce her, but I wouldn't.'

'Why not?' my friend asked.

'Oh, I dunno. I still loved her, I am still in love with her, I suppose. She might come back to me.'

'Would you divorce her now?' my friend said.

'I don't think so.'

'Not even if I asked you?'

'If *you* asked me?'

'You see,' he said, 'I was the other man and I wrote the

story, little knowing ... You were right about coincidences. I didn't have to fabricate a fall: I was always down and out, until she came. Perhaps my need is greater than thine, as Sir Philip Sidney didn't say. Without her, I should be—'

I got up. 'I'll think it over,' I said, 'I'll think it over.' I turned away blindly and in turning my foot caught in the fold of a rug and I went headlong. He helped me to my feet.

'Are you all right?'

'Yes, quite all right,' I gasped. 'But take care, and if she's anywhere about, don't tell her that I've had a real fall.'

A Very Present Help

DEIRDRE O'FARRELL (it wasn't her real name, though she was Irish) had been George Lambert's mistress for three years. She would have been his wife if he had had his way; but her position with regard to husbands, past, present and to come, was dubious. 'It's quite impossible,' she would say when he urged marriage on her; 'don't ask me why.' He didn't ask her; he accepted her and everything about her without question, and those elements in her make-up that were mysterious and unexplained had a particular glamour for him. Like a retriever carrying a handbag, he was proud of being the bearer of her secrets.

A younger man would have been more exacting. A more experienced man would have looked askance at Deirdre. He would have seen what there was to be seen: a very pretty face, rather chocolate-box, and eyes so blue that they seemed to create a bluish mist between them and the beholder. Through this mist her eyes shone with so much innocence that (to use a vulgarism) it wasn't true. But to George it was true. What gave life and character to her face was a kind of determination to make good. She was, in fact, a calculating little minx, a sexual tease and sometimes a sexual cheat. Every now and then she would withhold her favours, saying, 'Oh, no, I'm not in the mood'; or she would find some pretext for breaking an engagement at the last moment, leaving George with an evening to himself; sometimes she would even hint at other attachments which might be going to supersede his. This policy, however, she used with the utmost caution; she had almost a genius for knowing how far she could go.

During the first two years of their relationship, however, she could have gone any length and George would not have noticed. The idea that he was being made a fool of never entered his head, and wouldn't have influenced him if it had. There was a difference of eighteen years between them; he was forty-one when they met, and she, she said, was twenty-three. He was so much in love with her that his one desire was to satisfy her every whim. Indeed, her caprices only served to make him love her more, for they gave him unlimited opportunities for self-escape, which was, for him, his natural form of self-expression. On her he threw himself away with both hands. No neophyte in love with the love of God, and resolved above all else to do His will, could have got more satisfaction from self-sacrifice than George got.

His education in love had been a late development for two reasons, one psychological, the other material. By nature he was timid with women, and, though he wasn't aware of it, an aesthetic idealist, a connoisseur of looks. Plain women did not attract him, and pretty women whom, from some feeling of inadequacy, he associated with the fashionable beauties of the glossy papers, he felt to be utterly beyond his sphere. As well might a working-man think of going into the Ritz and ordering a cocktail, as George could think of being within arm's length of a beautiful woman. The working-man could do it, no one would prevent him, supposing he had the money and a decent suit of clothes, but equally nothing could persuade him to. The act was not impossible, but it was impossible for him. And so with George. The nimbus of glory that surrounded a pretty woman, added to the sundering effect of class, made her to him as unattainable as is the summit of Mount Everest to the average pedestrian. George knew that other men had scaled it, but knew that he could not.

The nearest he got to his divinities was to cut their pictures out and pin them to the wall—where he gazed at them with awe and reverence, and desire, but oh! how distantly.

Otherwise, he had not had much to do with women, for the second, the material factor in his late development was lack of funds. An only child, he had never mixed much with other children. His parents, who were dead, had scraped together enough money to send him to a small public school, but not enough to leave him any. He had a black-coated job in the City, and being conscientious, over-conscientious, as well as fearful for the future, his work came first with him. Too much so, in a way; for his preoccupation with doing it well made him miss opportunities for advancement which other men, with a keener eye to their own interests, and a wider range of vision, would certainly have seized.

So the legacy, the very substantial legacy from a distant relation which came to him at the age of thirty-nine, found him totally unprepared, socially, emotionally and mentally. Morally he was not so unprepared; his strong sense of obligation found immediate outlets: all sorts of people, and causes, could be benefited. The material aspect of his new position took him longer to realize: in fact he had to be told that with the money at his disposal he could buy himself a partnership in the firm—a proposal which, when it came, the firm welcomed with enthusiasm, for not only were they glad to have the money, they were glad to have him too, a modest, loyal, trust-worthy, hard-working man who had given them good service and no trouble. It could be truly said that no one grudged him his good fortune or the privileges that went with it—one of which was much more leisure, and another a widening range of social contacts.

It was not surprising that he found himself accepted in circles hitherto unknown to him. He was well-mannered, passably good-looking and undeniably eligible; and if he could not always tune in to the wavelength of the people he was with, didn't quite speak their language or understand its nuances, these social shortcomings were readily forgiven him; indeed they were rather welcome than otherwise, for they made him into a kind of pet, a well-meaning animal that has not quite been trained. Several women, one of whom had incidentally been his pin-up girl, undertook to train him and were tireless in trying to raise him in his own esteem. In this they were not altogether disinterested; for they realized that unless a man had a fairly good opinion of himself, he could not be what they would have him be. But the harder they tried, the more deeply they involved him in their silken webs, the more they increased his sense of obligation and apartness. What could he do in return for all this enveloping kindness? Little presents he gave them, flowers and trinkets, presents which were sometimes misunderstood; but rapturously as these tokens were received, they left him with a haunting sense of falling short. They were not enough! They were not enough! Mrs. de Sole, for instance, 'Délice' to her friends; after an evening in her drawing-room, with all its amenities of relaxation, conversation, and near-love, he felt he ought to carry her heavy luggage for her, for miles and miles and miles.

Actually he didn't find it easy to spend money; the penurious habits of his early life clung to him; he didn't think he ought to live beyond his income, the idea of spending capital appalled him. Gradually he reached a more realistic view of his financial position, and moved from his small house in the suburbs to a comfortable flat in South Kensington; but it was weeks before he felt he could afford it and months before he dared to give a party.

The party, however, was a success, for all those present were determined that it should be; and when the last guest left, George was left feeling that at last he had done something for somebody.

His men friends did not take the same view of George's potentialities that his women friends took. Their attitude might be described as coarser. They did not, of course, take the same trouble with him, but none the less they had their eye on him —the dark horse, the unknown quantity. Needless to say they didn't want to get him tied up in married life, but women came into their calculations. They thought of love in terms of money, not money in terms of love. At least, some of them did. Most of George's new friends were men who talked of money, and with whom money talked; they had chosen him, not he them; he didn't know his way about in this new world, and was both surprised and flattered when anybody showed an interest in him. The women he gravitated towards were of a gentler and more sensitive type than their husbands, they found George a pleasant change. But the men, being more objective and detached, summed up his position in some ways more accurately than they did.

'What you want, George, is a dog,' said one well-wisher, more discerning than the others.

'A dog?'

'Yes, something that would wag its tail when you come in, and lick your face.'

George thought about this.

'But I should have to take it out for walks.'

'Not all the time. You are such a glutton for responsibility. Sometimes it would look at you with huge pleading eyes, and then you could rub its ears and fondle it. A dog will absorb far more affection than a human being.'

'Do you think I'm affectionate?' asked George.

'In a frustrated way, yes, very. These women you go about with aren't much good to you, you're half-afraid of them. I'm not saying anything against them, mind, in their way they're tops, but not for you. They are too complex, you need something simpler, and more natural. A dog—'

'Yes?'

'Well, it would fawn on you and you could beat it.'

'What a horrible idea.'

'Or you could fawn on it and it would bite you.'

'Isn't there anything between the two?'

'Not for you, there isn't. No, you need a dog, with a strong emotional current uniting you. Not the sort of friendship you have with Mrs. Hake, or Halibut, or whatever her name is. She must freeze the pants off you.'

'I don't know who you mean.'

'That middle-aged harpy who gets you on a sofa and twangs your heart-strings with her varnished nails.'

'Oh, Délice de Sole! She's an angel.'

'That's what I mean. You need someone more fleshly, who would let her hair down, and help you to let down yours. We must arrange a party for you.'

That was how George met Deirdre. At the party were two other girls rather like her, and decidedly unlike the women that George was in the habit of consorting with. An atmosphere of good-fellowship prevailed. Champagne loosened tongues and George's feelings. As well as talking to him they talked at him and about him—the industrious apprentice who had made good and come into a fortune, the man who had the ball at his feet, the lucky chap whose name had got into the papers. Much of what they said was quite untrue but all of it was flattering, and even more intoxicating than the wine: under the admiring glances flashed at him, George began to feel the hell of a fellow.

Presently one of the other couples rose and the man, apologizing, said they had a date. 'We don't want to break up the party,' he added. 'That's all right,' their host said; 'Annette and I have a date too, at that new place, the Late Session; and it will be pretty late before we're back. But there's plenty more to drink; why don't you and Deirdre, George, stay on, and make an evening of it? It's only eleven o'clock. That is, if neither of you has a date?'

George and Deirdre exchanged glances. 'What do you think, Deirdre?' he asked. He didn't know her other name.

'I'm all for staying here,' she said.

'Well,' said their host, rising and taking Annette's hand, 'we couldn't be more sorry—it's too bad that it's turned out like this. But you will make yourselves at home, won't you? You know the geography of the house'—he waved his hand to indicate it—'at any rate Deirdre does. Goodbye, my children, don't get into mischief,' and he was gone, with his companion, almost before they had time to thank him for their lovely evening.

It was the first of several such evenings, some organized by George, to whom spending money was now becoming easy, even exhilarating. But he grudged sharing Deirdre's company; after the party he could have her to himself. Himself—his very self, only attainable in Deirdre's arms.

But no, it was attainable in other ways. Everything he did for her, every present, every treat he gave her, every wish of hers, expressed by her or anticipated by him, that he fulfilled, gave him, in a lesser degree, the same sense of wholeness and integration. He felt, and even looked, proud of being a man, and walked down Piccadilly with his hands in his pockets, looking as if he owned it. Even thinking of her, he was twice the man he had been. Only she could give him this freedom; with other women, the women he had known, he was still shy and diffident, anxious to please and sometimes succeeding, but always being acted on, not acting. Gradually he frequented them less and less; the silken threads by which they held him were a frail tie compared to the hawser which fastened him to Deirdre.

So for two years he was entirely happy. She could do no wrong for him. Her moods and caprices, the small slights and snubs, rebuffs and disappointments, by which she sought to make herself more precious to him, all seemed part of her; he scarcely distinguished between her melting and her stony moods. But then something in him became sensitized and if she was unkind to him it began to hurt. Now there were two Deirdres instead of one; and the second made him suffer. In vain he told himself that she had always been like that; it was unreasonable that something he had always taken for granted and not minded should suddenly become a grievance. He blamed himself more than her for his resentment, and was miserable until, at whatever cost to his pride and sense of fairness, he had made it up with her. He tried to make these tiffs and reconciliations into a habit, part of his emotional routine; an item on his experience account; but it didn't work out so. His feelings, instead of toughening, grew more tender; his eyes had a hurt, anxious look, which his other women friends, on the few occasions when he saw them, remarked upon. How quick they were to notice changes in him! He couldn't conceal from himself that he was unhappy; the joys of reconciliation and forgiveness (forgiveness of himself rather than her) became of shorter duration; soon, as an anodyne, they hardly counted. He was forced into making a distinction, which he had never made before, between her acts and her: Deirdre was one thing, what she did was another, so he told himself; but try as he would he couldn't keep them apart. It wasn't only the smart of the disappointments, which she was so expert in inflicting, that made him miserable; it was the nature that prompted them, his sense of which was like a smell that persisted even through her most fragrant and most yielding moments, and had something frightening about it: the smell of cruelty.

One evening at a party, a rather smart party that he had taken her to at her request, though not quite sure she would fit in, he suddenly felt ill—food poisoning or gastric flu—he didn't know what it was. He caught sight of his face in a looking-glass, and it more than confirmed what he was feeling. It wasn't easy to detach Deirdre from the young man she was talking to, but at last he did, and told her of his plight as well as he could, for by now the room was spinning round.

'I don't want to go now,' she said, 'I'm having a good time. You'll be all right. Get a hot-water bottle and go to bed.'

'Oh, do come back with me,' he begged her. 'I feel so odd, I don't know if I shall be able to get home.'

'Don't be silly,' she said. 'You know what an old fusspot you are. I'll look in and see you on my way back, if it isn't too late.'

He lay awake shivering and sweating, with his bedroom door open, hoping to hear her key turn in the lock, but he hadn't heard it when, towards three o'clock, he fell asleep.

His daily help was busy in the room when George woke up. He had had a dreadful night with bouts of vomiting and diarrhoea, sometimes alternating, sometimes simultaneous; and the blackness before his eyes, as he plunged across the passage to relieve them! Once he had to crawl. He didn't always get there in time, as his bedclothes bore witness.

'Never mind,' said the daily help, 'I'll change them for you. Don't try to get out of bed—I'll change them with you in it.'

He rolled from one side to the other, and somehow the distasteful task was done.

He could have had a servant living in, but most of his spare cash went to Deirdre, to keep her flat and her; for he had persuaded her, as much for his sake as for hers, to give up her secretarial work. With this she sometimes taxed him. 'You've taken away my livelihood,' she said.

She said, she said . . . Something that Deirdre had once said, and which he couldn't remember, was vexing George's throbbing brain when the telephone bell rang.

'Perhaps you'd rather I went away?' the daily woman

suggested. 'It may be something private.' He nodded weakly.

'Hullo, is that George? I didn't recognize your voice, you disguised it.'

'I'm laid up in bed.'

'Speak a little louder, can you?'

George repeated it.

'Oh, I'm sorry. I'll come round and see you. I couldn't come last night—it went on too late.'

'When will you come?'

'In half an hour or so.'

The morning passed; the daily help, who usually left at twelve o'clock, went out to buy some fish for his lunch—'I'll boil it for you,' she said.

George protested that he couldn't eat it.

'You must get something inside you,' she said, 'after all that vomiting.'

How kind she is, he thought, but the thought made him uneasy—she was doing something for him, meeting what she believed to be a wish of his—she was putting him in her debt, making him dependent on her. Receiving a favour, he felt uncomfortable. But Deirdre would be here any minute now, and for her he could do something—but could he, bedridden? He heard the click of the key turning—Deirdre at last! But no, it was the daily help again, for sounds came from the kitchen. At last the telephone bell rang.

'Darling, how are you feeling?'

'A bit better, thank you, but not much. When will you be round?'

'Isn't it too bad, I've been asked out to lunch, I may not get to you till tea-time. I'll make you some tea, but you'll have to tell me where you keep it.'

'I'm not sure if I know myself.'

'Oh, well, I'll find it. I must dash now.'

Presently the daily help came in, bringing the boiled fish on a tray, laid out very neatly. 'And I thought you might like some peas and potatoes.' His mouth watered at the sight of the food, but his stomach warned him, and he put the forkful down, while he tried to decide how serious the warning was. 'Hadn't you better have the doctor?' she asked. 'You don't look any too good.'

'Oh, I don't think so, you see my temperature is normal.'

'Well, try to eat a bit, and then have a nap and I'll come in and give you your tea.'

'It's very kind of you,' he said, 'Mrs. Buswell'—suddenly remembering her name. 'But Miss O'Farrell's coming in to do that. By the way, where is the tea kept?'

She always left the tea-tray ready when she went away.

'In the cupboard beside the fridge, on the second shelf. Well, bye-bye for now, sir, and I'll come later on and give you your supper.'

'How good of you,' he said. . . . But he didn't feel quite happy about the arrangement. He ought to have been giving her her supper.

Struggling with nausea he swallowed down some fish, picked at the peas, nibbled the potatoes; after an initial revolt, his stomach seemed to tolerate it, and, as often happens after eating, he felt better—well enough, in fact, to take the nap that Mrs. Buswell had recommended. (Was she taking one? He hoped so.) But when he woke he felt feverish and his sense of touch was out of order. Warm things felt cold; cold things felt colder; getting out of bed, wondering whether to be sick or not, he shivered in the August warmth. No matter, it was past four o'clock. Deirdre would soon be here.

Just at the moment when expectation had reached its peak, the telephone bell rang.

'Darling, it's me. I hate to disappoint you—if you are disappointed—but I've gone down to the country—it is so heavenly now, we're going to have a bathe—so I shan't be there to give you your tea. And I was so looking forward to it. But you'll be able to get it for yourself, won't you? And I'll come round in the evening.'

'What time?' George asked.

'Oh, any old time, but well before your bedtime. So long, my dear. Think of me taking a header. Ugh!'

She rang off.

George wrestled with his disappointment, but again and again it reared itself and struck at him, thriving on successive decapitations like a hydra. Even more than his body, his mind was troubling him, and if he tried to play off one against the other they united and made common cause against him.

He took his temperature. It was 101. He derived some comfort from the thought that his body was showing fight against the poison; but all the same he wished his temperature had been normal. Perhaps he had better call in the doctor. He dialled the number, only to be told that his doctor was away on holiday. Another doctor was attending his patients: would Mr. Lambert like to call him? In a frenzy of frustration George said no, then wished he hadn't, and sheepishly rang up again to ask the other doctor's number. Again his energy petered out; he couldn't bring himself to summon a strange doctor. He worked himself up quite a lot over this, then lay back and tried to relax and think it was another person suffering, not he—a device that succeeds, if at all, only when one is feeling nearly well. He tried various forms of mental consolation— that he wasn't bankrupt, that he was in bed, the proper place, not exposed in the desert being slowly devoured by ants, that he had friends who would be sorry for him if they knew. But would they be, when he had so shamefully neglected them?

This brought him back to Deirdre, who did know but didn't seem to be specially sorry. 'That's Deirdre all over!' How often had he used this phrase in her defence, in the days when what she was made anything she did seem unimportant. But now it didn't help.

If only she would come! The outside door opened and shut. Someone had come. 'Deirdre!' he called, as if by calling her name he could ensure that it was she; she must be Deirdre, if he said so. But it was Mrs. Buswell who came in, with the slightly resentful air of someone who has been called by the wrong name, a name, too, dearer than her own. Would he like some soup, she asked, and then a nice poached egg? George said he would; but wasn't it giving her a lot of trouble? Mrs. Buswell seemed a little put out, then smiled and said it was a pleasure to look after him. Slow as usual at taking in the idea that anyone could want to, George murmured excessive thanks. 'It doesn't do to be always giving,' she said cryptically. 'People impose on you. You should take as well as give.'

'Oh, but I take a lot!' said George. 'Not in the way I mean,' said Mrs. Buswell. 'And it doesn't do them any good, either.'

Wondering if it was what the doctor would have ordered, George ate his supper. He lingered over it, partly from loss of appetite, partly to eke out the interval before Deirdre came. Those long waits, with nothing but his thoughts to feed on! His thoughts were sicker than his stomach, or whatever part of him it was that had turned against him. Guiltily he remembered Mrs. Buswell. She would not go away, he was convinced, until he had eaten the last morsel. The last morsel took a great deal of getting down, but by swallowing it he felt he had done something for her, a little redressed the balance of mutual benefit. The look of satisfaction on her face rewarded him.

Swish, swish. Now she was washing up, and all for him. What a good creature she was! But he hoped she wouldn't still be there when Deirdre came.

She wasn't. She came in to bid him good night.

'I should take one of those red pills if I was you,' she said.

He was surprised that she knew what they were for, and that she took so much interest in his belongings.

'Would you give me the bottle?' he asked, for he did not keep the tablets by his bed, for fear he should forget how many he had taken. She brought them, and he shook out two, and handed her the bottle, which she replaced.

'I hope you'll have a good night,' she said, 'I shall be back again at seven o'clock.'

Seven o'clock! He hadn't realized she came so early; she lived in a distant suburb, and must get up at six. What a sacrifice, and all for him! He made an effort to accept the sacrifice as something due to him; but it didn't go down much more easily than his supper had.

He would take the pills, but when? He didn't want to be asleep when Deirdre came. Nine o'clock, ten o'clock, still she hadn't come, but then she kept late hours, and she slept late, too. He often had to wake her. It was one of the things he most looked forward to, her moment of returning consciousness. She was so young, it took her a long time to come to herself—and him.

How long should he give her? Till midnight, he decided; but when midnight came and he had taken the pills he didn't get off for a long time, for his unconscious mind, of which she had possession, kept nagging at him like a watch-dog.

Asleep at last, he dreamed, and dreamed of Deirdre, whom he had never dreamed about before; he had often wished he could. Having her he didn't need to dream of her; perhaps that explained it. He was back at the party where he had been taken ill. It was very like the original party, except that the lights were brighter and between the rugs the parquet floor was shinier. He was still asking her to go back with him, and the young man still waited impatiently and possessively at her elbow. 'Can't you see I'm busy?' she said. 'I'm trying to make a date with Rupert and you keep barging in.' Suddenly the floor tilted up, almost level with his eye, and he clutched at her to steady himself. 'Oh, do take care,' she said, 'you'll spoil my dress,' and he saw it was an oyster-coloured silk dress that he had given her, but not the one she had gone to the party in. 'Give him your arm, Rupert, I think he must be drunk.' The young man put out a helping hand but George shook it off. 'He's nothing to do with you,' he said to Deirdre, 'it's me you should be thinking of.' 'Can't you leave me alone one single minute?' Deirdre asked. 'I was just beginning to enjoy myself.' The room dipped and swayed, but somehow George managed to keep his feet. 'But you ought to come with me,' he said. 'You would come with me if you loved me.' At that both she and the young man laughed. 'Love you?' she said. 'I've never loved you, and now I almost hate you.' 'Never loved me?' said George, aghast. 'You mean to say you've never loved me, all this time?' 'No, of course not.' 'But I always thought you did.' 'What made you think so?' George became confused. 'Because ... because ... because I loved you, I suppose.' 'Yes, that's just it. You were so intent on loving me that you never asked yourself if I loved you. You never thought of my side of it, I never came into it except as somebody you were in love with. If you'd asked me whether I loved you, I should have told you no. It's the first question most men ask, but you didn't ask it because you didn't mind. You were in love with love, not me. If I'd existed for you as a person it might have been different, but I didn't. If you'd asked me to do something for you, except just one thing, it might have been different. But as it is—'

George reeled and crashed to the floor, and when he came to himself he was in fact on the floor, having fallen out of bed for the first time since he was a child.

He woke to a sense that something terrible had happened, but couldn't imagine what, for he himself felt better. But the thing would not let him enjoy his convalescence; it kept demanding to be known and recognized, and at last through a barbituric mist it forced its way.

Deirdre didn't love him, she had never loved him. She had appeared to him in a dream to tell him so, and the message was far more real and convincing than if she had spoken with her own voice, for it was the pure essence of experience, with no admixture of circumstance to dilute it. It was her spirit speaking straight to his—yes, straight, for she had told him straight.

It explained why she hadn't come back with him from the party, why she hadn't looked him up during the day, it explained everything that had puzzled him in her behaviour since first her behaviour began to puzzle him.

He felt he could not survive the blow, and the fact that he felt better physically made him better able to suffer mentally. He scarcely knew how to think, for all his thoughts that counted with him began and ended in Deirdre. Now they had nowhere to begin or end.

What time was it? It must be past seven, for through the square of glass over the door the light was shining, which meant that Mrs. Buswell had come back. He could not hear her, though. She must be taking great pains not to wake him. He called her and she came in, still on tiptoe.

'I was just going to bring you your tea,' she said. 'It's eight o'clock. Did you have a good night?'

George told her what had happened in the night.

'You fell out of bed! Poor Mr. Lambert! I might have known, the bedclothes are in such a mess. I meant to make your bed again last night, but thought you were too tired. Now when you've drunk this tea, see if you can get up and I'll make it for you. Or I'll make it with you in it. I do like to see a man look comfortable.'

'How kind you are.'

George found that he could stand without his head going round. While he was sitting in his dressing-gown the telephone bell rang. Mrs. Buswell, who was nearest, answered it. 'It's Miss O'Farrell,' she said, and a shadow crossed her face.

'Ask her to ring up later, Mrs. Buswell.' No sooner were the words out than he wished he could recall them.

'Mr. Lambert doesn't find it convenient to speak to you, Miss O'Farrell.'

What a way of putting it!

Expostulatory sounds came through the telephone.

'In about half an hour, he isn't well,' said Mrs. Buswell.

Torn between misery and a slight sense of relief at the reprieve, George watched Mrs. Buswell making the bed. The feeling that he ought to be making it for her, not she for him, was less pronounced than he expected. But soon another thought came.

'Why, it's Sunday! You ought not to be here on Sunday!'

'I came because you weren't well,' said Mrs. Buswell, 'and you were all alone.'

What a wonderful woman! George began to speculate about her. What was she really like? What had her life been like? He had never asked her. He had always taken her and her services for granted; he had never shown, or felt, any curiosity about her. He paid her, and that was all, unaware of the treasure hidden in her.

Back in bed he took his temperature. It was still a hundred, but health does not depend on the thermometer, and he felt definitely better.

The telephone bell rang.

'Good morning, darling. Who was that rude old thing who answered the telephone just now? She seemed to hate my guts.'

'The daily woman,' said George, stiffening.

'But aren't I your daily woman? I always used to be. But what I wanted to say was, How are you, darling?'

'Not very well.'

'You don't sound well, your voice sounds different. When can I come and see you?'

This was the crucial moment. George heard himself say:

'I don't think you'd better come. It may be something catching.'

'Some dreadful germ? Then perhaps I'd better not come. Oh, dear, and I do want to see you. Perhaps it's a good thing I didn't come last night. It was too late anyhow. We had such fun, though. I wish you had been there.'

'I was in bed.'

'I know, I know. Poor George! What luck you didn't give it to me, whatever it was. You can't have, or it would have come out by now, wouldn't it? Well, so long, darling. Let me know the first moment you're out of quarantine.'

George spent a miserable day. Why had he committed this ridiculous act of self-sacrifice and deprived himself of Deirdre's presence? It wasn't for her sake, or her health's sake, that he knew quite well; it was because—

Oh, hell!

A hundred times he made up his mind to ring her, and tell her he knew he wasn't infectious; a hundred times, prompted by the dream, he unmade it. He wondered if he was going mad.

He tried to distract himself by reading, but since he met Deirdre he had almost given up reading; she was his book, into which he had dipped deeper and deeper until, to change the metaphor, he was nearly drowned. How could a book, a mere commentary on life, give him what Deirdre gave him, which was life itself? Listlessly he turned the pages. What was paper as an interest, compared to flesh? What appeal to the heart had the printed word, compared to the voice that came from Deirdre's lips?

His loneliness increased, and with it the bitter self-reproach of having brought it on himself. He tried to attend to business; that was quickly done: at the office they begged him not to come back until he was quite well. Business: it had become automatic to him, second nature: he kept it in a compartment to itself, sealed off from his feelings. Sentiment in business: there was such a thing, but it was not the sentiment he needed.

Well, then, he had his friends, quite a number of them, for hadn't the catastrophe itself happened at a party where he knew almost everyone, though Deirdre didn't? Why not ring them up, and ask for sympathy?

One after another he went through their names; he even got out his address-book, in case he should have overlooked someone. Once these names had meant a great deal to him: they had meant the warmth of greeting, the exchange of ideas, the interplay of slight but real emotions. The reassurance of goodbye-to-meet-again, the sense, when it was over, that something had been added to the value of life. The value of life! But what did the value of life mean, in this tormented and bewildered age, when every value was being called in question? How did life benefit, or its values, if he and Mrs. Plastosell, of whom he was secretly a little afraid, she was so fashionable and so sophisticated, played an intricate game of cats-cradle on a sofa, gossamer webs spun out of airy nothings that involved some flattery on her side and a good deal of self-complacency on his? She condescended to him, and he lapped up her condescension: but he wasn't himself with her, not his true self: he played a part, half self-effacing, half self-advertising: she didn't liberate him, as Deirdre did. With Deirdre he could be absolutely himself and more: George plus, plus, plus, plus. With Mrs. Plastosell he was George minus, if he was anything.

He took up the telephone to dial her number: but when he had got half-way he put the receiver back.

'You ought to have the telly,' Mrs. Buswell said. 'Not all the time, like some people do, they're potty, to my way of thinking. But just for times like this, when you haven't anything to amuse you. It *gives* you something, that's the point.'

'I could have one,' George said.

'Well, it would take your mind off. And there are some quite good programmes. When my second husband died, and when my eldest daughter died, and when my son-in-law — that's the husband of my youngest daughter, or was, died — I don't know what I should have done without the telly. You see I depended on them, in a way. Not for money, of course. The telly made up for some of it.'

'I see,' said George, whom this catalogue of catastrophes had made a little ashamed of his own sorrow.

'Yes, it gives you something, if you see what I mean, it's like a present. Not that I'm against giving, far from it. I'll give with anyone, so far as I can afford it. But there comes a time when giving doesn't satisfy — you have to have something in return, if you take my meaning.'

'I think I do.'

'It isn't fair, and it's just as bad to be unfair to yourself as it is to be unfair to other people. You don't get anything out of being unfair to yourself.'

'No.'

'And they misunderstand and take advantage. They impose on you. It's happened to me, before now, poor as I am. Not with my relations, though, I will say that.'

'I'm imposing on you now,' said George. 'I'm taking advantage of your good nature.'

'No, you're not. I'm glad to work for you.'

'But what do I give you in return?'

That's stumped her, George thought.

'Oh, I dunno. I suppose I like seeing you around and then we have a chat together sometimes. And then you pay my wages.'

'That isn't much,' said George.

'And then I'm sorry for you.'

'Because I'm ill?'

'That, and other things.'

What did she mean? She knew about his relationship with Deirdre, of course; she couldn't help knowing. But she couldn't know about his dream and how it had upset him.

'For everything you've done for me,' he said, 'I'm more than grateful. Tell me something I can do for you and I'll gladly do it.'

'You just lie still and get better,' she said. 'Then you'll have done something for me. And take a tip from me, sir, though it's not for me to give it. You'd be happier without that Miss O'Farrell hanging round.'

During the next few days the telephone bell rang many times and each time George answered it in a different spirit. Desire, despair, grief, anger—anger lasted a long time: how dared she not love him when he loved her, and had done so much for her—given her the life she never could have had without him? Now he was like a nut whose kernel has been eaten by a worm; he could almost hear himself rattle. The emptiness, the dryness! No current could recharge him; the battery was worn out. He could never go through all this with another person, the expense of spirit had been too great. The expense of spirit in a waste of shame: had it been that? Were the moralists right to warn you against the sins of the flesh? Most of his friends believed, and he too had believed, that the senses fed the mind and nourished the affections; without their co-operation the spirit withered, but if so, why was he in this plight—mentally, emotionally and spiritually bankrupt? With no friends, no interests, no hopes, just an abyss, a void, where Deirdre had once been?

Then came revenge. Ah, he would show her! Hate was a

E

stimulant as well as love; he would get the same satisfaction from hating her that he had once got from loving her, the same delight from thwarting her wishes that he had once got from granting them.

'Darling, I didn't recognize your voice.'

'You say that every time you ring me up.'

'But every time it's true.'

It probably was true, for every time they spoke on the telephone he had a different feeling for her: now it was hatred, and hatred speaks with a different voice from love.

'But darling, you can't *still* be infectious! It's four days now.'

'But you're so frightened of infection.'

'Yes, but I could put my head in through the door.'

'I shouldn't like to think I'd given you something.'

'But you've given me so many things! I shouldn't mind one little tiny germ.'

'Let's put it off another day. It would be safer.'

'Darling, it must be as you wish.'

In spite of the joys of hatred, he suffered agonies each time he said he would not see her. And hatred disagreed with his digestion. All his life he had been delicate, suffered from headaches, bronchial asthma and attacks of fibrositis; during the three years he had been in love with her all these had disappeared; he had a clean bill of health. But now no longer. The symptoms of food poisoning, or whatever it was, had gone, but he still didn't feel himself. All his processes, mental and physical, were disorganized. He flourished on agreement. The spirit of opposition, denying his deepest impulses their outlet, was making a sick man of him. He forgot little things, was constantly mislaying his belongings—sometimes he couldn't see them when they were staring him in the face, a sort of amnesia of the eye—and his daily routine, the order in which he did things, got hopelessly confused. He cleaned his teeth with shaving-soap and tried to shave with tooth-paste. What would happen at the office, where he was due back on Monday?

'Take her back! Take her back!' said the voice within him that always pleaded for her; 'take her back, and let things go on as they used to! She is no different now from what she was; she was always like this, only you didn't know it! Can't you re-establish the relationship on the basis of truth? Truth is antiseptic, it will cleanse and heal the wound, and then when she behaves in character you won't be angry, because you know what makes her tick! You were in love with a false Deirdre, created by your imagination; aren't you man enough to love the real one, now that you know her faults? She loved you, knowing yours—women are more realistic than men—'

'But she didn't and doesn't love me, that's just it.'

'How do you know?'

'Because she told me so in a dream.'

'A dream! What sort of evidence is a dream?'

Then followed a part of the record that George was altogether too familiar with—the pros and cons of the dream. But hadn't her subsequent behaviour verified it, hadn't Mrs. Buswell's hints and ultimate outspokenness confirmed it?

Without Mrs. Buswell he would have given in, for every time that he forgave Deirdre (and in his heart he forgave her seventy times seven) he felt so much better physically and mentally, so nearly restored and integrated, that sometimes he would snatch up the receiver and start to dial her number. 'Darling, I'm quite all right: do come round now!' Mrs. Buswell was never present when he committed these extravagances, but her invisible presence restrained him from fulfilling his intention. Regretfully he put the receiver back.

It was the vision she had given him of reciprocal affection dominating, softening, yes, and even sweetening, physical love.

Physical love, she must know all about it, a working woman who had had two husbands. But she insisted on reciprocity: she didn't think that love was healthy without it. 'But surely, Mrs. Buswell' (so he argued with her shade), 'unselfish, unrequited love is the noblest of all emotions? The love that religion itself enjoins on us—the love that expects no return?' But she wouldn't have it. 'God himself,' she said (in these imaginary conversations), 'wouldn't expect us to love Him unless He first loved us.'

On Saturday the telephone didn't ring; the morning passed and still it didn't ring. At lunch-time when people are most likely to be in, George rang Deirdre.

'Welcome 9191.'

'Hullo, darling, does that sound more like me?'

A pause, some readjustment at the other end, he couldn't tell what.

'Yes, it does, it does sound more like you.'

'Well, what about coming round to see me? I'm not catching now. You could even kiss me if you wanted to.'

'Of course I want to, but . . .'

'But what?'

'Well, I'm engaged this afternoon.'

'Then come at drink-time.'

'Yes, if I can manage it.'

He had brought himself to the point of not expecting her when Deirdre came.

'Darling, of course I'm glad you're better but I should be gladder still if you hadn't been so cruel to me.'

'Cruel to you?' George repeated, when, after some hygienic holding back, their kiss was over. But his conscience smote him: he had been cruel, or had meant to be.

'You said you were too ill to see me, but I think you were shamming.'

'If you had come to see me you would have known I wasn't.'

'To begin with, perhaps. Then you said you didn't find it *convenient* to speak to me—such a nasty way of putting it.'

'Mrs. Buswell said that.'

'I don't care who said it—it came through your mouthpiece, and all the time I was in agonies, wondering what was happening to you.'

'You were having a bathe when I was worst.'

'You couldn't expect me to stay indoors all day, George dear, just because you had a tummy upset. And you've always said you wanted me to enjoy myself.'

'Oh, don't let's bicker,' George said. 'You're here now, that's the great thing.'

'Yes, in the end you sent for me, just as if I was some sort of call-girl.'

'Oh, what nonsense you talk.'

'It isn't nonsense at all—you've changed towards me. You don't love me any more.'

'What?' said George, and his heart missed a beat.

'You don't love me any more, and that's why I've done what I've done.'

'What have you done?' asked George, and a nameless terror clutched him.

'First tell me you're truly sorry, and then I might not do it.'

'But you said you had done it.'

'Well, I have and I haven't. If you said you were sorry and were really nice to me—'

George took her in his arms.

'—then I might change my mind. But I don't think I shall, because, you see, I know that you don't love me.'

'I do love you, I do love you!'

'No, or you wouldn't have played me up like you did. That's why I decided—'

'What did you decide?'

'I oughtn't to tell you because it has to do with someone else.'

'Who?'

'Now you're asking.'

Sounds came from the kitchen—it was Mrs. Buswell, his ally, come to cook his supper.

Something stiffened in him.

'Of course I'm asking, and I wish you wouldn't treat me like a child.'

'It was only because I didn't want to hurt you.'

'Hurt away,' said George. 'You can't hurt me more than you have hurt me these last few days.'

'Don't you think I can?'

'Just try.'

'Well, darling, since you must know, though you can't say I haven't warned you, it's Rupert.'

'That man at the party?'

'Don't call him that man, darling, he's very well off and very nice to me. He said he'd like to—'

'Well?'

'See a lot more of me. Don't misunderstand me—we're just great, great friends, that's all.'

Mrs. Buswell, in the kitchen, was making quite a clatter. George released Deirdre and got up shakily.

'Then go to him,' he said.

Deirdre turned her large eyes on him, those eyes that stained with blue the intervening air, and suddenly he saw the fear behind them. 'You don't mean that, treasure, do you? You don't really want me to go to Rupert?'

'You can go to hell for all I care.'

'Oh, but sweetie-pie, you wouldn't like that, would you? You wouldn't like to hear me sizzling, because you would be there, too, because in a way, you know, you seduced me—it wasn't nice of you. And I've been with you all these years, as everybody knows. If you send me to Rupert—'

'I'm not sending you.'

'If you let Rupert have me—'

'It was your idea, not mine.'

'Well, you'll be lonely, won't you? You won't find another girl to make things as easy for you as I have. You're shy, you know—you haven't much self-confidence with a girl when it comes to the point.'

George said nothing.

'And you know you've messed my life up—the best years of my life. You've trailed me around and put a stigma on me—Rupert won't like that.'

'But you said he wanted you to go to him.'

'Yes, darling, he does, but I don't want to—not very much, that is. Of course he loves me and I could get to love him—'

'Well, why not?'

'Because I love you better, oh, much better.'

What a racket Mrs. Buswell was making in the kitchen!

'You don't love me,' George said. 'You told me so yourself.'

'I told you so? I never. You must have dreamed it.'

'Well, if I did, it's true, and you must go now.'

'Go? Go where?'

'Out of this flat.' And taking her arm George began to propel Deirdre to the door.

'Oh, but how can you be so cruel? I haven't anywhere to go to—only my own rooms, that you pay for. Oh, what shall I do? It wasn't true what I told you about Rupert—he doesn't want me, and I don't want him. I only said it because you were so unkind to me.'

'Get out of here, get out!'

'How can you turn me away like this, when you've been so fond of me and done so much for me? You've always been so good and generous—'

'Get out —get out!'

The door shut out the sound of Deirdre's sobbing. George

sat for what seemed a long time, looking at his knees, then round the room, then at his knees again. Like everyone who has taken violent action he was unable to comment on it.

There was a knock at the door.

'Come in,' he said, hardly knowing whom he was going to see.

'She's gone,' said Mrs. Buswell.

'I thought she went half an hour ago.'

'No, she didn't, she stayed on the landing, outside the door. She rang once or twice but you didn't hear and I wouldn't let her in—I said you were resting. Of course she didn't dare to use her key. I should get it back from her, if I was you. You never know. She's gone now.'

'Oh, dear, Mrs. Buswell.' The 'dear' might have been for her, or part of the exclamation. 'What do you think about it all?' Somehow he took it for granted that she knew what had been happening.

'I say good riddance to bad rubbish.' She looked with compassion at his working face. 'Don't take on, sir, she's not worth it.'

George wasn't so sure; he didn't know how to feel, and it seemed incongruous, disproportionate, almost incredible that the emotional experience of three years could be ended by one small act of violence, lasting only a minute.

Much later in the evening, after Mrs. Buswell had gone, he went to the telephone and dialled a number.

'Can I speak to Mrs. de Sole?'

'Speaking. But who is that?'

'George Lambert, Délice.'

'*George?* I didn't recognize your voice.' Would his voice never be the same again? 'You *are* a stranger. Well, when can we meet?'

'Could I come round and see you now, or is it too late?'

'It's never too late to mend. I'm not clairvoyante, but I suspect you want to tell me something.'

'Don't be hard on me, will you? I've just been rather hard.'

'On yourself, no doubt.'

'No, on someone else.'

'Well done, I congratulate you. But you won't find me hard
—I shall be softer than silk, snow, swansdown, anything you
can think of.'

E*

A High Dive

THE circus-manager was worried. Attendances had been falling off and such people as did come—children they were, mostly —sat about listlessly, munching sweets or sucking ices, some-times talking to each other without so much as glancing at the show. Only the young or little girls, who came to see the ponies, betrayed any real interest. The clowns' jokes fell flat, for they were the kind of jokes that used to raise a laugh before 1939, after which critical date people's sense of humour seemed to have changed, along with many other things about them. The circus-manager had heard the word 'corny' flung about and didn't like it. What did they want? Something that was, in his opinion, sillier and more pointless than the old jokes; not a bull's-eye on the target of humour, but an outer or even a near-miss—something that brought in the element of futility and that could be laughed at as well as with: an unintentional joke against the joker. The clowns were quick enough with their patter but it just didn't go down: there was too much sense in their nonsense for an up-to-date audience, too much articulateness. They would do better to talk gibberish, perhaps. Now they must change their style, and find out what really did make people laugh, if people could be made to; but he, the manager, was over fifty and never good himself at making jokes, even the old-fashioned kind. What was this word that everyone was using—'sophisticated'? The audiences were too sophisticated, even the children were: they seemed to have

seen and heard all this before, even when they were too young
to have seen and heard it.

'What shall we do?' he asked his wife. They were standing
under the Big Top, which had just been put up, and wondering how many of the empty seats would still be empty when
they gave their first performance. 'We shall have to do something, or it's a bad look-out.'

'I don't see what we can do about the comic side,' she said.
'It may come right by itself. Fashions change, all sorts of old
things have returned to favour, like old-time dances. But
there's something we could do.'

'What's that?'

'Put on an act that's dangerous, really dangerous. Audiences
are never bored by that. I know you don't like it, and no more
do I, but when we had the Wall of Death—'

Her husband's big chest-muscles twitched under his thin
shirt.

'You know what happened then.'

'Yes, but it wasn't our fault, we were in the clear.'

He shook his head.

'Those things upset everyone. I know the public came after
it happened—they came in shoals, they came to see the place
where someone had been killed. But our people got the needle
and didn't give a good performance for I don't know how
long. If you're proposing another Wall of Death I wouldn't
stand for it—besides, where will you find a man to do it?—
especially with a lion on his bike, which is the great attraction.'

'But other turns are dangerous too, as well as dangerous-
looking. It's *being* dangerous that is the draw.'

'Then what do you suggest?'

Before she had time to answer a man came up to them.

'I hope I don't butt in,' he said, 'but there's a man outside
who wants to speak to you.'

'What about?'

'I think he's looking for a job.'

'Bring him in,' said the manager.

The man appeared, led by his escort, who then went away. He was a tall, sandy-haired fellow with tawny leonine eyes and a straggling moustache. It wasn't easy to tell his age—he might have been about thirty-five. He pulled off his old brown corduroy cap and waited.

'I hear you want to take a job with us,' the manager said, while his wife tried to size up the newcomer. 'We're pretty full up, you know. We don't take on strangers as a rule. Have you any references?'

'No, sir.'

'Then I'm afraid we can't help you. But just for form's sake, what can you do?'

As if measuring its height the man cast up his eyes to the point where one of the two poles of the Big Top was embedded in the canvas.

'I can dive sixty feet into a tank eight foot long by four foot wide by four foot deep.'

The manager stared at him.

'Can you now?' he said. 'If so, you're the very man we want. Are you prepared to let us see you do it?'

'Yes,' the man said.

'And would you do it with petrol burning on the water?'

'Yes.'

'But have we got a tank?' the manager's wife asked.

'There's the old Mermaid's tank. It's just the thing. Get somebody to fetch it.'

While the tank was being brought the stranger looked about him.

'Thinking better of it?' said the manager.

'No, sir,' the man replied. 'I was thinking I should want some bathing-trunks.'

'We can soon fix you up with those,' the manager said. 'I'll show you where to change.'

Leaving the stranger somewhere out of sight, he came back to his wife.

'Do you think we ought to let him do it?' she asked.

'Well, it's his funeral. You wanted us to have a dangerous act, and now we've got it.'

'Yes, I know, but—' The rest was drowned by the rattle of the trolley bringing in the tank—a hollow, double cube like a sarcophagus. Mermaids in low relief sported on its leaden flanks. Grunting and muttering to each other the men slid it into position, a few feet from the pole. Then a length of hosepipe was fastened to a faucet, and soon they heard the sound of water swishing and gurgling in the tank.

'He's a long time changing,' said the manager's wife.

'Perhaps he's looking for a place to hide his money,' laughed her husband, and added, 'I think we'll give the petrol a miss.'

At length the man emerged from behind a screen, and slowly walked towards them. How tall he was, lanky and muscular. The hair on his body stuck out as if it had been combed. Hands on hips he stood beside them, his skin pimpled by goose-flesh. A fit of yawning overtook him.

'How do I get up?' he asked.

The manager was surprised, and pointed to the ladder. 'Unless you'd rather climb up, or be hauled up! You'll find a platform just below the top, to give you a foot-hold.'

He had started to go up the chromium-plated ladder when the manager's wife called after him: 'Are you still sure you want to do it?'

'Quite sure, madam.'

He was too tall to stand upright on the platform, the awning brushed his head. Crouching and swaying forty feet above them he swung his arms as though to test the air's resistance. Then he pitched forward into space, unseen by the manager's wife who looked the other way until she heard a splash and saw a thin sheet of bright water shooting up.

The man was standing breast-high in the tank. He swung himself over the edge and crossed the ring towards them, his body dripping, his wet feet caked with sawdust, his tawny eyes a little bloodshot.

'Bravo!' said the manager, taking his shiny hand. 'It's a first-rate act, that, and will put money in our pockets. What do you want for it, fifteen quid a week?'

The man shook his head. The water trickled from his matted hair on to his shoulders, oozed from his borrowed bathing-suit and made runnels down his sinewy thighs. A fine figure of a man: the women would like him.

'Well, twenty then.'

Still the man shook his head.

'Let's make it twenty-five. That's the most we give anyone.'

Except for the slow shaking of his head the man might not have heard. The circus-manager and his wife exchanged a rapid glance.

'Look here,' he said. 'Taking into account the draw your act is likely to be, we're going to make you a special offer— thirty pounds a week. All right?'

Had the man understood? He put his finger in his mouth and went on shaking his head slowly, more to himself than at them, and seemingly unconscious of the bargain that was being held out to him. When he still didn't answer, the knot of tension broke, and the manager said, in his ordinary, brisk voice,

'Then I'm afraid we can't do business. But just as a matter of interest, tell us why you turned down our excellent offer.'

The man drew a long breath and breaking his long silence said, 'It's the first time I done it and I didn't like it.'

With that he turned on his heel and straddling his long legs walked off unsteadily in the direction of the dressing-room.

The circus-manager and his wife stared at each other.

'It was the first time he'd done it,' she muttered. 'The first time.' Not knowing what to say to him, whether to praise, blame, scold or sympathize, they waited for him to come back, but he didn't come.

'I'll go and see if he's all right,' the circus-manager said. But in two minutes he was back again. 'He's not there,' he said. 'He must have slipped out the other way, the crack-brained fellow!'

The Crossways

ONCE upon a time there were two children, called Olga and Peter, and they lived on the edge of a huge forest. Olga was nine and Peter was seven. Their father was a woodman and very poor. Their mother's name was Lucindra. She came from another country; their father had met her in the wars. She was beautiful and had fine golden hair. Though she was sometimes dreamy and absent-minded and would suddenly speak to them in her own language, which they didn't understand, she was very fond of them and they loved her.

But Michael their father was a stern man and they were both a little afraid of him. Even Lucindra was afraid of him, for when he was angry he would scold her and sometimes tell her he wished he had never married her. And when this happened she wished she had never married him, but she did not dare to say so; besides he was strong and handsome and could be kind and loving when his fits of bad temper were over.

One thing he had always told his children, they must never on any account go farther into the forest than where they could still see the sunlight shining through the edges. The trees were so thick and the paths so few and hard to follow that even the foresters themselves sometimes lost their way. And there were dangerous animals as well, wolves and bears and wild boars. Michael still carried a scar from a gash that a bear had given him; it ran all the way from his elbow to his shoulder, making a bluish groove in his skin which you could feel with your finger. When he wanted to impress on them the danger of going too far into the forest he would show them the scar. Olga used to try not to look at it but Peter said he would like to have one like it.

Michael would not let even Lucindra wander about in the forest alone, though sometimes he took her with him when he went out with his horse and cart. Then they would eat their dinner together under the trees, and she looked forward to that. But he usually went on foot, for the road soon came to an end and branched off into footpaths which lost themselves among the trees. So she did not know much more about the forest than the children did. But like them she wanted to know more, for their cottage was miles away from any town, and sometimes weeks passed without her seeing anyone.

One afternoon, however, when Michael was away at work, a stranger called. He was a young man, slight and slim, with hair as fair and eyes as blue as hers, which was not surprising for he came from her own country and had heard of people whom she knew. He was a pedlar who sold bead necklaces and brooches and bracelets and ribbons. These did not interest Peter very much but he also had pocket-knives and scissors and many other things. He brought them all out of his bag and laid them on the table in the kitchen which was their living-room; they shone and glittered and suddenly the whole place seemed much more cheerful, though Lucindra kept shaking her head and saying she was much too poor to buy anything. The young man said he didn't expect her to, but he went on bringing more and more things out of his bag, even after it looked to be empty, and he was so gay that soon they were all laughing, Lucindra most of all; the children had never seen her laugh like that. And finally she went out of the room and came back with some money, and bought a bracelet for Olga and a pocket-knife for Peter and a necklace for herself. Then she told the young man he must be getting on his way, otherwise it would be dark; and he laughed and said he was in no hurry, because he knew the forest quite well. But greatly to the children's disappointment she would not let him stay. So, telling her how unkind she was, he began to gather together his bits and pieces and put them back into the bag. The children could not take their eyes off him as one by one he packed the treasures away; and every now and then, if something was specially pretty, he would raise his eyebrows as though inviting them to buy it; but each time Lucindra shook her head. 'You must go, you must go,' she kept saying. 'All in good time,' he answered and looked slyly at the children, who knew that he was delaying his departure on purpose. But at last he got up and swung his sack over his shoulder and they followed him to the door where his horse was nibbling the grass; and he fixed the sack on a sort of pannier on its back and jumped into the saddle and wished them goodbye.

'Which way are you going?' Lucindra asked.

'To the Crossways,' he answered, smiling down at them.

'Where's that?'

'Don't you know?' They didn't, and then he told them that in the heart of the forest there was an open space where many roads met; 'and one of those roads,' he said, 'leads to the land of your heart's desire.'

'But how would anyone find the place?' Lucindra asked.

'Easily,' said the pedlar. 'Just follow the full moon until you come to it.' He pointed upwards and there was the full moon hanging low over the forest.

'But how do people know which road to take?' Lucindra asked.

'Oh, it's marked with a signpost,' said the pedlar. He laughed again and rode off, and they went back into the house, which seemed very dull and empty.

Soon after that their father came in and the children at once began to tell him about the pedlar. They were still very excited and could think of nothing else, for they had never had such an adventure in their lives before. 'Did you see him in the forest?' they asked. 'I saw no pedlar,' he answered frowning. 'I believe you dreamed the whole thing.'

'Oh, no, we didn't. Look, look, look.' And disregarding their mother's warning glance they showed him the bracelet and the pen-knife, and made Lucindra go and fetch her necklace, for she had already put it away. When he saw the necklace he grew still more angry and upbraided her bitterly for spending so much money. 'We're hard up as it is,' he said, 'and you must needs go buying things from this smooth-tongued scoundrel. Never let me see you wearing them.' Peter and Olga began to cry, and their mother let the necklace slip through her fingers on to the floor. 'If ever I catch him I shall know what to do with him,' Michael said. So they never told him the rest of the story or spoke of the pedlar any more.

It was a hard winter and it set in early, but in spite of that people did not seem to want wood as they used to, and Michael grew more and more morose and sour. Often when he came home he would not speak to them at all, and sat apart brooding, or went out again mysteriously and did not come back till after midnight. There was no pleasing him. If they sat quiet as mice he would complain of their silence; if they talked he would tell them to shut up. This was not so bad for the children as it was for their mother, for they now went to the village school and so had company. It was a long way to walk but they enjoyed it; they felt free the moment they got out of the house, and rather dreaded coming back, to find their mother drooping and listless, and their father, if he was at home, not lifting his head when they came in. Sometimes they lingered and talked to their friends, but they never spoke of the state of things at home, because they had promised their mother not to.

One evening they had stayed away later than usual and were

beginning to feel hungry and look forward to the hot, steaming supper their mother always prepared for them; so in spite of everything they found themselves longing for the moment in their homeward walk when they could first see the light shining through the windows. But there was no light and when they got into the house it was empty. They called and called but nobody answered, so they began to feel rather frightened and went out of doors again. It was much lighter out of doors because there was a moon.

'It's a full moon,' whispered Peter to Olga, 'like that evening the pedlar came.'

They went back into the house and found some matches and lit the lamp, and felt a little more cheerful, for it showed them their supper keeping warm on the hearth. They did not go to bed when they had eaten their supper; they sat in chairs like grown-up people. But Peter had gone to sleep before their father came in.

'Where's Cindra?' he said in a thick voice. (He called her Cindra sometimes.) 'I asked you, where's Cindra?' Peter woke up and began to cry. They told him all they knew. 'But she can't be gone,' said Michael disbelievingly. 'She wouldn't leave us.' He got up and went into the bedroom and stayed there a long time. When he came back his hand shook and he was so pale that his hair looked quite black. 'It's true,' he said, 'she has gone. I found a letter. She says I'm not to try to follow her. She's gone where her heart calls her. What shall we do? What shall we do?'

When Olga saw that he was frightened she suddenly felt sorry for him and much less frightened herself.

'Don't worry,' she said. 'We know where she's gone to, don't we, Peter?'

'Where, where?' their father asked, his eyes darting at them.

'To the Crossways.'

'Nonsense,' he snapped. 'There is no such place.'

'Yes, there is,' said Olga patiently, 'in the middle of the forest. You can find it by following the full moon.'

'The full moon!' he echoed scornfully. 'I know every inch of the forest and I tell you there isn't any Crossways.'

'Please, please don't be angry,' Olga begged him. 'Let Peter and me go, if you don't believe us.'

'Let you go,' he said, 'and lose you too? Haven't I told you that the forest is dangerous? Do you want to send me mad? Sit still and don't stir from here till I come back.'

He went out and they heard him calling 'Cindra! Cindra!' until his voice died away.

'There's only one thing to do,' said Olga. 'We must find her and bring her back.'

'But what about the bears and the wild boars?' said Peter.

'Oh, I shouldn't worry about them,' said Olga. 'I'd much rather you went with me, of course, but if you're afraid I'll go alone.'

This made Peter feel much braver and they started off. They met with no difficulty in finding the way, for the moon made a pathway through the leafless trees; and at first they were not at all frightened, for when they looked back they could still see the light in the cottage windows. They walked hand in hand and their feet made a pleasant rustling on the fallen leaves.

'Will she be pleased to see us?' Peter asked.

'Of course she will, we're her children,' Olga answered.

'But suppose we don't find her at the Crossways?'

'Then we must go on until we do find her. The signpost will say which way she went.'

Whiter and whiter grew the moon as it swung into the heavens, and colder grew the air.

'I don't think I can go on much longer, Olga,' Peter said.

'You can if you try.'

It was then that they saw the bear. It was walking on all fours when they saw it, but when it saw them it stood up.

'Oh, it's going to hug us!' Peter cried.

'Nonsense,' said Olga, but her voice trembled. 'Perhaps it'll give you a scar like the one Daddy has,' she added, hoping to encourage him.

'I don't want a scar now,' sobbed Peter.

'All right,' said Olga. 'I shall just tell it why we've come.'

She went up to the bear and explained that they were looking for their mother, and the bear seemed satisfied, for after swaying a little on its feet and shaking its head, it got on to all fours again and shambled off.

After this escape they both felt very much better, and as if nothing could now go wrong. And suddenly they found that they were not walking on a path any longer, but on a road, a smooth straight road that led right out of the forest. On either side the trees seemed to fall back, and they were standing on the edge of a great circular plain which the moon overhead made almost as bright as day.

'Now we shall soon see her,' Olga said. But it wasn't quite so easy as she thought, for the plain was dotted with small, dark bushes any one of which might have been a human being; and Peter kept calling out, 'Look, there she is!' until Olga grew impatient.

They saw the Crossways long before they came to it. It was shaped like a star-fish, only a star-fish with fifty points instead of five; and the place where they met was like white sand that has been kicked up by the feet of many horses.

But their mother was not there and they walked slowly round the centre, looking at each signpost in turn to see which led to the Land of Heart's Desire. But not one gave any direction; they were all blank, and presently the children found themselves back at the signpost they had started from.

Then in the silence they heard a little sound like a moan, and looking round they saw their mother, lying in a hollow beside the road. They ran to her and she sat up and stretched her arms out and kissed them many times.

'We've come to fetch you back,' they said.

She smiled at them sadly. 'I can't come back,' she said. 'You see, I've hurt my foot. Look how swollen it is. I've had to take my shoe off.' They saw how swollen her foot was, and it was bleeding too. 'You'd better go home, my darlings,' she said, 'and leave me here.' 'But we can't leave you,' they both cried. And Peter said, 'Look, there are some people coming. They will help us.'

He ran towards them crying, 'Please help us', but they paid no heed and did not seem to see him. One after another they found the signpost they were looking for, and went the way it pointed, laughing and singing.

'They can't see us,' Lucindra said, 'because they are going to the Land of their Heart's Desire, and we don't belong to it.'

Then both the children felt cold and frightened, much more frightened than when they had met the bear.

'Couldn't you walk if you leaned on both of us?' Peter asked. She shook her head. 'And how should we find the way?' she said. 'The moon won't help us to go back.'

They lay down beside her, clasping her in their arms, and tried to keep awake, for the cold was making them drowsy. Just as they were dropping off they heard a footstep coming down the road; they did not pay much attention for they knew they would be invisible to whoever came. But Olga roused herself. 'I'm going to try again,' she said, and standing up she saw a long shadow like a steeple, and in front of it a man, walking very fast.

'Oh, Daddy, Daddy!' she cried. But his eyes were wild and staring, and bright with the empty shining of the moon. Terrified lest he too should not recognize them, she seized his hand. He stopped so suddenly that he nearly fell over.

'Where is your mother?' he cried.

'Here! She is here!'

She pulled at his hand, but he shrank back when he saw them, and without looking at their mother he said, 'Cindra, I came to say goodbye.'

'But it isn't goodbye,' cried Olga. 'We want you to take us home.'

He shook his head. 'No, no,' he said. 'I have been unkind to her. I am not worthy of her. She must go where she wants to go.'

'But you must take her, you must!' Olga besought him. 'Look at her, she has hurt her foot and can't walk.'

For the first time he brought himself to look at her, and went up to her and wonderingly touched her foot.

'Do you really want to come with me?' he asked.

'Yes, yes,' she murmured. 'But do you know the way?'

'I know the way all right,' he said with a touch of his old arrogance, and stooping down he lifted her in his arms.

Suddenly they saw written on the signpost, which had been blank before, 'The Land of Heart's Desire'.

It pointed straight back the way they came. And the moment their feet were turned towards home they began to laugh and sing, just as the others had.

Per Far L'Amore

THAT August in Venice, an August between the wars, the mosquitoes were particularly poisonous and voracious. Even the Venetians, who are usually immune, being inoculated against these pests, sometimes appeared with reddened wrists and swollen faces. Nor did the insects abide by their own rules; they did not wait for twilight to begin their feasts; they bit by day as well as by night. Hotel proprietors and their staffs, even while covertly scratching themselves, would not admit that there was anything abnormal in the visitation; 'E la stagione,' they would observe philosophically: 'It is the season.' Most Italians take comfort in the thought that manifestations, however unpleasant, are following a natural order, and are apt to say they are, even when they are not. But the visitors to Venice, waking with puffy eyelids and twisted bumpy lips, after perhaps many an hour spent crouching or kneeling under their mosquito-nets, trying to make their bedside lamps shine into the dark folds where the mosquitoes lurked, were not so easily satisfied, and many of them took wing like their tormentors, and flew to mountain resorts, which were said to be above the mosquito line. The only section of the community who profited from the outbreak were the chemists, who did a roaring trade in oil of citronella, small coloured candles guaranteed to suffocate mosquitoes, and other forms of insect-bane; it was before the days of Flit and DDT. But their triumph was short-lived for they were soon sold out—not only of preventives against the bites but even of remedies for them, and were reduced to fobbing off their customers with sunburn lotions and beauty preparations which, so they declared, would have the same effect as antiseptics.

To add to this misfortune a heat-wave of almost unexampled virulence struck the city. Indeed, it struck the whole Italian peninsula. Every day the local paper, the *Gazzettino*, and the national papers, the *Corriere della Sera* and the *Stampa*, published a list showing the maximum and minimum temperatures of all the large towns in Italy, including Benghazi which then formed part of the Italian empire. Benghazi was always top with upwards of 40 degrees Centigrade; but whereas of the others, Rome, Milan, Naples, Florence and Bologna always had a maximum temperature higher than that of Venice, which never rose above 35, Venice always had the highest minimum temperature, for it never fell below 26. Shallow and tepid, the lagoon, which had no chance to cool off, embraced the city like a permanent and inescapable hot-water bottle. Sometimes the more mathematically minded of the English and American tourists, those who were still capable of making the effort, might be seen at some café table, pencil in hand, making the complicated calculation that reduces Centigrade to Fahrenheit. 'Ninety-four today,' they would lament, 'one degree lower than yesterday, but the humidity is greater—eighty-nine per cent, only two degrees less than in New York.'

The nights seemed hotter than the days. In the afternoon the wind would veer from north to south, from the borino to the scirocco, and by six o'clock—the one tolerable moment of the day—it would be blowing lustily: the visitors snuffed it up, auguring each other a cool night: but by eight o'clock the breeze would have died down, and then the baking pavements and lukewarm canals gave off all the heat they had stored up during the hours of sunshine. Later the full moon would show its rim, fiery as a conflagration, behind the island of San

Giorgio Maggiore, and slowly mount until the whole of its great disc, blood-red, and swollen as if it too had been mosquito-bitten, would rise above the roof-tops. Clouds surrounded it and sometimes streaked it, indigo clouds edged with rose, like the clouds in Tintoretto's pictures, making the hopeful think a storm was brewing; but they were only harbingers of heat, and presently the moon swung clear of them and climbed into the dark vault of the night, losing as it went its ruddy hue, changing from copper to amber, and at last to shining white, a waxen death-mask pitted with blue shadows.

Dining late on the terrace of his hotel, against which the ripples of the Grand Canal lapped softly, Mr. Henry Elkington watched it, while he waited for his wife and daughter who, however late the hour, were always later. The terrace was the coolest place, as cool as any spot in Venice, he imagined; yet he felt the sweat collecting on his forehead and saw it glistening on the backs of his hands. Every now and then it would trickle stealthily down his chest and he knew, though he could not feel it, that it was also coursing down his back, for when he leant against the upholstered chair and then leant forward, the chair stuck to his white linen coat. A dark patch must have formed there, an unsightly mark and one that would leave a stain; but at fifty-odd he didn't mind that as he would have minded twenty years ago. He minded the discomfort more, however, and grudged the physical effort of flipping at the mosquitoes. Guided to him unerringly by the red-shaded table-lamp, as by a beacon, they announced themselves with a venomous ping—where were they exactly? His face and head and hands he could to some extent defend with whirlwind gyrations like those of a demented windmill; but his calves and ankles, which were their happiest hunting-ground, those he could not protect. And, tired by sleepless nights, his mind kept telling his sense of self-preservation that it would be better to give up the struggle, adopt a policy of appeasement and let the little creatures have their fling.

Apart from all this he wasn't feeling well; he had some psychosomatic disorder that made his flesh creep even when the mosquitoes were not stinging it. He felt as though his skin didn't quite fit him, it was loose in some places and tight in others; and much as, in one way, he welcomed every breath that blew, another part of his sensorium shrank from it. He was hot and cold by turns; perhaps he had a fever.

Hope stirred in him, however, for his wife, before she went to dress, had promised she would ring up Countess Bembo and say that after all they were afraid they would not be able to stay on for her party, two days hence. He, Henry, was not well, that was to be the excuse: the mosquitoes and the heat had got him down, and the three of them were departing on the morrow for the Dolomites. The Dolomites! The mere word, with its suggestion of fresh mountain air, mosquito-free, breathed new life into him and he called the waiter for another dry martini.

He had had the greatest difficulty in persuading Maureen to take this step. Not that she was, normally, indifferent to the needs and even the whims of a husband who had given her almost everything she asked of life, except romance. She knew what was due to such a husband, and she did not grudge it him. But this was a special case. Countess Bembo was an important Venetian hostess, perhaps the most important, and her party was to be one of the highlights, perhaps the highlight, of the season. It would be a thousand pities to miss it. For herself she, Maureen, would not mind; but Annette would be so terribly disappointed. Annette was only twenty and it was her first visit to Venice. Venice had gone to her head; she could find no flaw in it. She wasn't worried by the heat and the mosquitoes, she thought them rather fun — part of the tremendous fun she was having at the endless parties to which she was invited. Young men buzzed round her—Henry could not keep count of the Nino's and Nini's and Gigio's and Gigi's, or tell them apart, they were as like each other as mosquitoes; but he had to admit that they were good-looking and had excellent manners, and Annette obviously found them far more interesting and exciting than the young men she knew in England. Sailing, bathing, playing tennis, dancing, she went off with them for hours at a time. Henry was slightly worried by these absences, but Maureen seemed to know exactly how far her daughter should be chaperoned, and would draw the line, or not draw it, in circumstances that to Henry's thinking were precisely similar. One thing had always been clear: no conjunction of circumstances whatever must be allowed to prevent Annette's attendance at the Bembos' party.

This was the first time for days that they had dined alone. Annette was her father's darling as she was her mother's and Henry would not have dreamed of depriving her of a pleasure if he had not felt that his health was at stake. Those newspaper paragraphs grew every day more frequent: 'Colto da malore', struck down by sudden illness, this or that middle-aged man (they all seemed to be in the decade between fifty and sixty) had fallen down in the street and been taken to hospital, where he had either instantly expired or been adjudged curable in (at the least) twenty days. Sudden death or three weeks' confinement, three weeks' grilling in a Venetian hospital! Henry, who was of a full habit, trembled at the thought. Now, looking out at the Venetian night, at the gondolas passing below him, dipping and prancing, at the whole medley of small and large craft, hung with lanterns, some silent, some with solitary singers, some with concert parties thrumming mandolins, he tried to recapture the fascination, the sense of heady joy, that the scene had once held for him. But now it spoke to him of nothing but the wish to get away and slake his suffering, sweltering body in the cool air of the mountains.

There was a touch on his shoulder, light as a mosquito settling, and he looked up into Annette's radiant face. 'Mummy's just coming,' she said.

This was not quite true. Maureen appeared about ten minutes later. Henry could not tell from her expression what the verdict was to be: Maureen seldom introduced an important topic until the conversation had turned on other matters. Then unobtrusively she would slip it in. While they confidently munched their scampi and Henry was toying with his grilled sole, Maureen remarked:

'I didn't forget to telephone to Loredana Bembo, Henry dear.'

Hope surged up in him.

'Oh, and what did she say?'

'She couldn't have been sweeter about it. First she said she was frightfully sorry you were feeling the heat—she sent you all sorts of affectionate messages.'

Henry's heart sank.

'And she said she entirely understood your wanting to go away. She wished she could herself. But Henry, she *implored* us not to fail her. She said that so many people had chucked —because of the heat, you know, and the mosquitoes—that it would hardly be a party at all—about thirty people for dinner at the most. She said that except for us there wasn't a cat in Venice.'

'I'm not sure that I like that,' said Henry with a feeble attempt at jocularity.

'Well, you know what she meant. And it is hard on her, isn't it, when she's made so many preparations. And she said the nicest things about Annette. I really don't think we could let her down now—do you, darling?'

'Perhaps not,' said Henry doubtfully.

'And oh, Henry—I nearly forgot—she said you needn't be afraid of the mosquitoes because there wouldn't be any. She's thought of the most amusing way of keeping them out. She thought of it entirely for you, she said. It's to be a secret until the evening of the party.'

Henry realized that there was nothing for it but to give way with a good grace.

Somehow or other he managed to survive the next two days, but not unscathed, however. Taking his morning stroll to the flower-shop in San Stefano (he had to renew the flowers in their sitting-room every day, for after twenty-four hours they had wilted from the heat) he suddenly felt dizzy: the sun seemed to strike right through him, like a sword, as if the proper defences of his body had ceased to operate. 'Colto da malore'! In a panic he looked about for shade but there was none: the sun stood right over the long, acorn-shaped campo. Then he espied an awning and staggered to it. Standing in its exiguous shadow he felt as a shipwrecked man might feel on a rock, with the ocean raging round him. But where next? Frightened though he was, he didn't want to risk the moral defeat of going back without the flowers: besides, Maureen would be so disappointed. Half-way to the shop a projecting doorway lent a modicum of shade. He gained it, and gaining it regained some of his lost confidence. It was all nerves! But no, it wasn't, for scanning the campo he saw other pedestrians pursuing the same policy as his; avoiding the torrid centre where the statue was, they were slinking round the circumference, hurrying from one island of shade to the next. Still, none of them dropped down dead, and soon he plucked up courage, and almost swaggered into the flower-shop, where the flowers were being sprayed with jets of water and the sudden coolness was unbelievably delicious.

But he didn't go out again that day till after sundown, and the next day, the day of the party, which dawned as hot as noon, he gave the flowers a miss and didn't go out at all until their gondola drew up to the brass-railed landing-raft and

Maureen said to the gondoliers, 'Palazzo Bembo, sa!' as if, on that evening, there could only be one destination.

Casa, Maureen should have said; house, not palace. In some ways the Bembos were old-fashioned, and affected the nomenclature of an earlier day than that in which the houses of patrician Venetian families came to be styled palazzos. Theirs was one of the few ancestral homes in Venice inhabited entirely by the family who built it, and kept up in appropriate state. This evening that state had been much augmented. If there was not a powdered footman on every step of the grand staircase, there were a formidable number, all the same; and if they were not professional footmen, but farm-workers imported from the Bembos' country estate and put into livery, the effect was none the less magnificent. Passing them on the staircase, and vaguely noting their white-gloved hands and red, perspiring faces, Henry felt that afflatus of the spirit which earthly glory sometimes brings. Other Venetians gave parties that were like parties everywhere; but the Bembos' party had its special cachet.

Light-headed but heavy-footed he stumbled, and clutched at the plaited rope of crimson silk that, threaded through stylized hands of polished brass, hung in festoons against the wall. Good luck! said somebody. A step or two ahead of and above him were Maureen and Annette: what energy was displayed in their sprightly, springy tread! His ankles were swollen under his black socks, and the slight exertion of climbing the staircase was bringing the sweat out on his back.

In an ante-room off the *sala* stood Loredana Bembo, an imposing figure, splendid in jewels, and by her side her husband, a short, thickset, baldish man, but with an unmistakable air of authority about him. 'It was so good of you to come,' she said to Henry. 'And I promise you a hundred lire for every mosquito-bite you get tonight.' A hundred lire was something in those days; it will pay me to get a bite or two, thought Henry, and waited for the buzz, but it didn't come, and when at last they all sat down to dinner, he saw why; the windows were defended by thin metal grilles, of mesh so fine that even a mosquito couldn't find its way through. He had seen them before, of course; his own sitting-room in the hotel was fitted with them. They couldn't be the secret Countess Bembo had spoken of.

He wasn't sitting next to her, an ambassador and a man of title occupied these coveted positions. Of his two neighbours, one was an Italian, one an Englishwoman who always came to Venice at this time.

'What is Countess Bembo's secret?' he asked her. 'Or haven't you heard of it?'

'There is something,' she said.

'Do you know what?'

She shook her head. 'Loredana always has something up her sleeve,' she said. 'Let's hope it won't be too peculiar.'

A member of one aristocratic Venetian family, married into another, Loredana Bembo was a law unto herself. Conventional when she chose to be, if the fit took her she would flout convention. At such times a reckless look would come into her eyes. 'E originale,' her friends said of her, 'she is an eccentric,' and if they sometimes criticized her they were also proud of her and a little afraid. What she said went, what she did got by.

The champagne flowed, and as fast as Henry drank it his labouring, overheated skin discharged it. He dabbed his neck, his face, his hands. Perhaps it would have been wiser not to drink, but he could not forgo the momentary relief each swallow brought him—the immediate physical relief, and the deliverance from his nervous premonitions. All nerves they were: tomorrow this time he would be at Merano breathing freely. Drinking freely he could better imagine that paradise.

F

The faces opposite him were a blur, but one was Maureen's, and another, farther to the left, between a Nino and a Gigi who were both talking to her at once, was Annette's.

At last the chairs scraped on the smooth *terrazza* and they left the dining-room, in Continental fashion, the men and women together, a little group of white shirt-fronts and bare shoulders. Up they went, upstairs into the second *sala*, for the Palazzo Bembo had two, two great galleries that ran the whole length of the building. Breasting the ascent, however, they stopped, as a crowd stops, automatically, almost barging into each other: and little cries broke out and circled over Henry's head. 'Ah, che bello!' As they moved on and up, these exclamations, and others like them, screams and trills and chirrups of delight, went on, and Henry, reaching the top, saw what it was that had provoked them, though for a moment he didn't quite take in what it meant. He blinked and looked again: what was it, this array of snowy surfaces, booths, tents, tabernacles, this ghostly encampment under the great chandelier? Then, drawing nearer, he saw: it *was* an encampment, an encampment of mosquito-nets. Following the others' lead, Henry began to circulate among them. They were of all shapes and sizes, some square, some domed and circular, some tapering to a peak like army tents. To one and all gaily coloured pennons were attached, indicating their purpose. Under the chandelier, where the light was brightest, was pitched a cluster of square tents meant for bridge, as their label, 'Per far una partita', testified. Beyond them, farther from the light, round and square forms alternating, were other tents reserved for conversation: 'Per far la conversazione' was the device they bore. Beyond them, where the light was fainter, was ranged another group, only big enough to hold two armchairs apiece: 'Per far l'amore' was the legend that these temptingly displayed. A gasp went up; had Loredana gone too far this time? And beyond these again, one in each corner of the room flanking the tall gothic windows, where the light from the chandelier hardly reached them, almost out of sight, were two much smaller refuges. These at once aroused the curiosity of the guests: what could their purpose be? They peered and peered at the labels, which were not coloured or cut into fantastic shapes, but sober rectangles of white cardboard, with plain black lettering on them. Then there was a chuckle, which sooner or later was taken up by everyone: 'Per i misantropi', they read, and soon the words were on every lip.

The first tents to be occupied were the bridge tents: the impatient players made straight for them, and within a minute or two the cards were being dealt. If some of the guests were too slow off the mark, and lost their places at the bridge-tables, they concealed their disappointment and joined the conversationalists. One or two paired off, and somewhat sheepishly and defiantly made for the tents of love: cries of encouragement followed after them. As far as Henry could make out, no man or woman chose to be self-proclaimed a misanthrope: the two lone tents remained unoccupied. But he had scarcely time to see, for it was like a game of musical chairs—one had to find one's seat or be left standing, and the idea of standing was much less bearable to Henry even than the idea of talking. 'Per far la conversazione!' There was a vacancy: in he went and sank down in a chair. There were iced drinks in misted glasses on the table, and round it three people whom he knew quite well: it might have been much worse.

He it was who drew together the tent-flaps and tied them with gay bows of scarlet ribbon: if the tents were not mosquito-proof, as he suspected, they looked as if they were, which was a great thing: he could relax, he needn't flap and flip, and screw his face up, or make other uncivilized gestures of the mosquito-ridden. Outside, no doubt, the creatures hummed, they must, for at both ends of the *sala* the windows stood wide open, and with two glittering chandeliers to guide them they couldn't miss their way. No, it wasn't too bad. The muslin kept out some of the air, of course, but how clever of Loredana to have thought of it all! She had turned those twin plagues, the heat and the mosquitoes, neither of which was funny in itself, into a joke. She had converted them into a social asset, she had countered them with a creation that was beautiful and strange. The party would be long remembered.

Fuddled though he was, and ready to accept unreality, Henry began to wonder where, in what muslin arbours, Annette and Maureen had taken shelter. The first question was quickly answered. Faintly, from below, came the strains of a dance-band.

'You didn't know?' said someone. 'They're coming in after dinner to dance, a whole crowd of them. It's we old-stagers who are sitting up here.' He was an Italian and *vecchietti* was the word he used: 'a little old', such a nice word, there was no equivalent for it in English, we were less considerate to old age. Henry didn't mind being a *vecchietto*. So Annette was accounted for: she would be downstairs dancing with a Nino, or a Nini, a Gigio or a Gigi. She would be sure to be enjoying herself.

But Maureen? He looked about him. Even here where the light from the chandelier was fairly strong, you couldn't very well see through the muslin; you could see the shadowy shapes of other tents, but you couldn't tell who was inside them; in the case of those farther away, nearer the windows, you couldn't tell if anyone was inside them. Maureen was so efficient, so practised socially; she would have found her niche—not with the bridge-players, for she wasn't one, not—he smiled to himself—in one of the *temples d'amour*, for that didn't interest her—she would be taking part in another conversation-piece, perhaps next door to his. While with the surface of his mind he gossiped with his fellow guests his inner ear was alert for the

inflexions of Maureen's voice; and so intent was he on listening that he didn't see the figure that more than once passed by
his curtain wall, stopping and peering in and circling round;
and it was one of the others who first saw her and said,
'Guardi, Enrico, isn't that your wife who goes in search of
you?' At once Henry jumped up and excusing himself untied
the ribbons and let himself out into the air.

'What is it?' he said, moving with her into a space between
the tents that was out of earshot. 'Anything I can do?'

'Darling, I've got a splitting headache,' she answered. 'I
really think I must go back. It came on suddenly—it's the heat,
I suppose. But I don't want to spoil Annette's fun, she's having
the time of her life, and I don't want Loredana to know, she
has so much on her hands already. So I'll just slip out—she'll
never notice—and Luigi and Emilio can take me back to the
hotel.'

'I'll go with you,' Henry said.

'No, darling, don't do that. What I should like you to do,
if you don't mind, is to wait for Annette and bring her home.
When you go you can explain to Loredana and make my
apologies. I know it's a frightful bore and you're not feeling
well either—but just this once! It really wouldn't do to let
Annette go back alone, we know she can be trusted but people
would talk about it. I hate to ask you to, but it won't be for
long—what time is it?'

'Just twelve,' said Henry. 'There's the Marangona.'

They listened, and above the hubbub of voices and dance
music they heard the solemn sound of the great bell tolling
midnight.

'I won't tell Annette that I'm going,' Maureen said, 'and
don't you tell her either; it might spoil her fun. I'll send the
gondoliers straight back and tell them to wait for you. Now
we mustn't be seen talking together any more or it will look
odd.' Before Henry could speak she had turned away, and with

slight inclinations of her head to left and right was making for the staircase.

Henry made a movement to follow her and then turned back. She knew her own mind, no one better. But what should he do? Irresolutely he looked towards the tent he had left—but was it the same tent? He couldn't be sure, and anyhow another man had taken his place, leaving the flap open. Several of the tents had their flaps open, the occupants preferring air and light to freedom from mosquitoes. He picked his way among the tents. Which one should he invade? They all seemed full. Even the bowers of love, which were more opaque than the others, had darker shadows in them. He was shut out! For a moment he felt as a wandering Arab might, whose tribe had exiled him. But he mustn't stand there moping: he would go down and watch the dancers.

Plenty of other guests were doing the same: on gilt chairs and settees they lined the walls; behind them the crimson brocade stretched upwards to the ceiling of painted beams; pictures and mirrors hung above them. His tired mind could not synthesize the scene. Better try to find Annette—ah, here she was, on the arm, or in the arms, of a young man. Her face was rapt and expressionless: she passed within a foot of Henry without seeing him. She was in another world, a world of youth into which he could not penetrate—a world which jealously guarded its own feelings, especially from lonely wallflower fathers. The music whined and groaned and thumped and stammered. Where was she now? There were other rooms, rooms for sitting out in, that led off the *sala*. He mustn't seem curious about her, he mustn't feel curious about her, she didn't belong to him, she belonged to all those young men, the Nino's, Nini's, Gigio's and Gigi's, and the emotions they aroused in her: emotions which sometimes made her youthful face look stern.

Here she was again, on another arm, this time; and this time her face was not so much rapt as set, and in the lines of her body there was the tautness of strain, such as you see in a plant that is being forced to grow in a shape it doesn't like. Was she a captive? He thought her eyes met his: he longed to say, 'Oh, please come here and talk to me a moment!' But he must not; if she had been in another continent she could not have been farther from him.

At most times she could see a joke as well as anyone, indeed she often laughed when he saw nothing to laugh at. But where her young men were concerned she was, it seemed to him, as impervious both to humour and to reason as her mother was in matters of social etiquette and observance. She took it all with deadly seriousness, even when she was laughing and flirting with her swains; and she resented any comment on her conduct, however sympathetic and well meant.

'Does she really know what she is doing?' he had once asked her mother. 'She seems to think that love today is different from love at any other time.'

'Oh, Annette's all right,' Maureen replied. 'Besides, there's safety in numbers. We mustn't interfere, we must let her find her feet. If she was really serious about anyone, I should know.'

'Yes, but this isn't England,' Henry said. '*Autres pays, autres mœurs.*'

Maureen shook her head. 'We mustn't spoil her fun,' she said. It had become a slogan.

Henry did not like watching people dance, it pricked him with nostalgia and a sense of guilt that he, too, was not dancing; so after a while he went upstairs again. This time he spied a breach in one of the muslin fortresses: it widened, a head emerged and a voice urged him to come in. He obeyed. The flap was folded to, the bows were tied, the outside world withdrew. But it was only a brief respite. The other man of the trio looked at his watch: 'Why, it's two o'clock,' he said.

'Dobbiamo filare—we must be off!' The warmth and gracious-
ness of their farewells made Henry feel more lonely than before.
Again he descended to the ballroom, this time he would risk
Annette's displeasure, beard the Nino's and the Gigio's and
beg her to come back. 'Your mother isn't well!'—that should
be his plea. But this time he couldn't see her in the milling
throng; she had vanished: face after beautiful face looked
blankly down at his. Perhaps Loredana knows where she is, he
thought, and diffidently approached his hostess where, fresh
and animated as five hours ago, she sat, magnetizing the men
on either side of her: but just out of range of her conscious
glance he stopped. With a hundred or more guests about her,
how could she know where Annette was? And it would be a
clumsy, tactless question anyway; how Annette would hate the
notion of a search-party, of being run to earth! And he might
have to explain, prematurely, about Maureen, too. So he waved
to his hostess as gaily as he could, and she shouted something
out to him: Venetians always shouted at you—in ballrooms as
well as from bridges—something he couldn't catch: was it
good night? Did she think he was taking his leave? Making it
as inconspicuous as possible? He couldn't tell, and slowly,
availing himself of the silken rope, he climbed to the upper
gallery.

It was in semi-darkness; in the splendid chandeliers only a
few lights sparkled. Had all the non-dancing guests, the
vecchietti, departed? The encampment hadn't been dismantled;
nothing had been put straight: the servants had left the task
of tidying till the morning. Peering in, he saw the cards scattered on the card-tables. The more distant tents, the bowers of
love, he could hardly see, still less tell whether they were
tenanted. He passed by them towards the windows and saw,
with a sudden rush of longing, the two tents set apart for the
misanthropes. Either would be a refuge. He chose the farther
one, in the darker corner; once inside, he felt rather than saw

that he was its first occupant. Draw the flaps and make them fast; let the mosquitoes sing outside! Dimly the thud and whine of the music reached him; it had no power to disturb him now: it was a lullaby. Soon he fell asleep.

He dreamed and in his dream he was still looking for someone, but it wasn't here, it was in the bright sunshine among the bathing-huts and cabins of the Lido. The search was most embarrassing, for all the cabins had their blinds drawn down, and every time he knocked an angry voice said, 'Who's that? You can't come in.' 'I'm looking for my daughter, Annette,' he explained. 'She's a tall girl, dark, and rather pretty. I want to take her home. Have you seen her?' 'We have seen her,' the voice replied, 'but she doesn't want to go home, and she'll be angry if you try to find her. Nino and Nini and Gigio and Gigi are looking after her. She has her own life to live, you know.' 'Yes,' said Henry, 'but her mother is anxious about her. She doesn't want her to go home alone—it wouldn't do. People would talk about her. Please tell me where she is.' 'She's somewhere here,' the voice said grudgingly, 'but you won't be able to get in because the door's locked. This is a *temple d'amour*, so please leave us in peace.'

Oddly enough Henry knew at once which door the speaker meant and went straight to it. But now he was carrying some flowers, flowers he had bought in the Campo San Stefano that morning, and he was glad of this because they gave him an excuse. He knocked and said very humbly, 'Please let me in, Annette, and don't be angry with me: I've only come to give you these flowers—you can wear them in your hair or anywhere you like, but you needn't wear them at all if you don't want to. Not everyone likes flowers.' But though he knew she was inside she didn't answer, and he saw that the flowers were withering in his hands.

He wasn't really asleep, he was only dozing, and the dream kept repeating itself in other sets of circumstances which were

F*

much less clear than they had been in the first one, until at last the visual aspects of the dream grew indistinct and only the sense of frustrated search remained.

When he awoke he thought he was in bed, his own bed with the mosquito-curtains round him. Gradually he remembered, and his first sensation was one of relief: he had outwitted Time and all those boring hours of waiting, they had slipped past his tired consciousness and now Annette would be ready and perhaps waiting to be taken home—and not best pleased at being kept waiting. He must go to her at once. For a moment that seemed as easy as it would have in a dream: then full awareness of his situation dawned on him. He was here in the Palazzo Bembo and it was quite dark: too dark to see his wristwatch. He struck a match: it showed a quarter to five. He let himself out into the open, and as his eyes got used to the darkness saw around him the ghostly forms of the encampment, looking strangely large and solid. No sound came from any part of the building. He had been forgotten, that was it. The ball was over and in the general concourse of goodbyes his absence had been overlooked. Someone would have taken Annette back; it only remained for him to go back too.

All this was something to be thankful for. But when he began to think about his situation, it didn't seem so simple. To begin with, how was he to get out of the house? And how, if discovered, would he explain himself? Would he be mistaken for a burglar? And how would he get home? Annette would have taken the gondola. He would have to walk, and he wasn't sure he knew the way.

He went to the window and leaned out. It looked on to a garden, a square garden, quite large, one of the few gardens in Venice. Dawn was not far away: he could see the Renaissance pavilion at the end, the shadows of night still dark between its columns. Nothing stirred, though he could hear the plash of the fountain in the centre. Would he have to go through the garden to get out? He had never approached the Palazzo Bembo on foot. Somewhere, he supposed, there must be a narrow *calle*, an alleyway that led to the main street. But where?'

Baffled, he turned away from the window and, treading cautiously between the tents—afraid of catching his foot in one and tearing it down—he made his way to the other end of the great *sala*. Light met him as he went, the accumulated radiance of the lamps of the Grand Canal. He leaned out of the window, and drank in the familiar scene. How beautiful it was—Venice asleep! Perhaps this was the only hour out of the twenty-four when no one was abroad.

His roving, loving eye at last looked downwards. Moored to the blue *pali*, which looked curiously foreshortened from above, was a gondola. The gondoliers, in their white ducks and blue sashes, were asleep: one curled up on the poop, the other stretched out in the hold: each was using his curved arm as a pillow. Whose gondola could it be? Why, it was his—his gondola, with Luigi and Emilio in it. But why were they there, why hadn't they gone home to bed?

A solution occurred to him. If they had taken Annette to the hotel, as they must have, probably accompanied by some cavalier—Annette's young men always accepted a lift—she might have sent them back to fetch her father. She would have looked for him, no doubt, before she left. But would she? Assuming she had remembered him at all, would she not have concluded that he had left the party earlier, with her mother, and dismissed the gondola when she reached the hotel? Or could it be that the party wasn't really over and she was still somewhere about?

He stole downstairs into the lower *sala*. All was in darkness there, but he sensed its disarray—the debris of the party without the party spirit. His flesh creeping as if from contact with something dirty, he returned to the upper *sala*, and on an

impulse shouted down the palace wall, as loudly as any
Venetian could have:

'Luigi!'

When he had repeated it a few times there was a movement
in the boat, and with sighs of escaping sleep, almost as loud as
steam, the gondoliers rose to their feet and looked incredu-
lously upwards.

'Have you seen the signorina?' he shouted in Italian.

'Nossignore.'

'Didn't you take her home?'

'Nossignore.'

'How did she go home then?'

'She must have gone on foot.'

She might have done, but was it likely? Telling the gondoliers to wait—for waiting, even more than rowing, was their
métier—he tried to work it out. She might have thought it fun
to walk, but would she have forgotten the gondola? Except
where her boy-friends were concerned, Annette wasn't inconsiderate. It would have been very inconsiderate to leave Emilio
and Luigi out all night.

His musing steps had brought him back to the encampment.
Unwillingly he re-entered its precincts. How alien it was. Like
something conjured up by an enchanter—purposeless, yet with
a potent personality of its own, and not a pleasant one: a personality that recalled the lawless deeds of desert warfare. He
was careful not to brush against the muslin fabrics. Each tent
had its flap ajar—all the birds had flown. But no, one tent was
shut. As though by compulsion he approached it. It was shut,
and there were two other odd things about it. The tent was
laced as tightly as a shoe, but the scarlet bows were tied on the
outside, not the inside; and its pennon had been torn off, torn
roughly off, for where the join had been a dark rent showed,
and if he peeped through it—

He didn't peep but stood at gaze, obsessed more deeply every moment by a sense of momentousness that was totally devoid of meaning. If, as he felt it might, the secret, the solution, lay inside the tent—

It did lie inside, sprawled over the two chairs, but he would not let himself believe, and here the darkness helped him; for it wasn't growing lighter with the opening day, it was going back to night. Needing air and a moment to confirm his unbelief he staggered to the window, the one that overlooked the garden, and there he saw the massy thundercloud piled high against the light and heard without heeding it the rumble of the storm that was to end the heat-wave. The lightning flashed and flashed again; the mirrors on the walls reflected it; a sudden gust blew in—a solid wall of wind that struck the tents and bent them all one way, like spectres fleeing. A flash lit up the whole length of the *sala*. He could not shirk his duty any longer, his duty as a man and as a father. Something might still be done to help, to reanimate, to bring back— But nothing could be done; around the darkening neck the scarlet fork-tailed pennon had been tied too tight. Another flash told him no more than he knew already: but the next lit up the legend on the noose. Two words were missing, hidden by the strangler's knot, but the operative word was there, the last one, and his memory supplied the rest: *Per far l'amore,* to make love.

Interference

AFTER his tenants had left, Cyril didn't try to replace them: let their rooms stand empty for a while, he thought.

They had never been unoccupied before, or not for long, since Cyril bought the house twelve years ago. Then the Gooches had them, the couple who kept house for him; it was only when they left to better themselves that the rooms fell vacant. Cyril couldn't afford another couple; the ministrations of the daily woman, helped out occasionally by the gardener, Mr. Snow, who had his own flat at the top of the house, must suffice his needs. But the housing shortage pricked Cyril's conscience; the empty rooms, that echoed to his tread, were to his spirit like a cold hot-water bottle on his flesh; they chilled it. Hence the tenants, who had no service obligations and who paid Cyril instead of being paid by him.

Five rooms they had, two bedrooms, a bathroom, a sitting-room and a kitchen. Awkwardly placed, they didn't constitute a flat or a maisonette or any sort of dwelling you could give a name to. The kitchen and the sitting-room were self-contained and had their own entrance, a green door giving on the garden, invisible from Cyril's part of the house. One went downstairs to them, as if to a basement, but it wasn't really a basement: their windows looked out on the garden, not on an area wall, for the house, being perched on a steep slope, had an extra storey on the garden side, making four in all.

What a strange house it was. Built on to at different times, it had no plan or method. Few of the eighteen rooms were on the same floor-level as the others; a step up or a step down led to them. The architects, it must be admitted, hadn't wasted any space on passages or landings; door followed door with a suddenness that confused strangers. In the days when Cyril had visitors to stay they often lost their way—indeed it was some time before Cyril could find his. Some of the rooms were roughly pentagonal in shape, with the doorway in the short fifth wall: should the door happen to be open, you got an oblique view of the room—you took it by surprise—walls meeting, pieces of furniture sidling up to each other—all most irregular.

The tenants' bedrooms and bathroom were also self-contained, behind a door that shut them off from Cyril's domain. But between them and the sitting-room was a tract of common ground—a section of the staircase that, winding its way up from below, made a brief halt outside the tenants' door. Only eight steps impaired their privacy, but sometimes Cyril met the Trimbles on them. 'Unlucky to cross on the stairs,' he would say gaily, and it always seemed to amuse them.

Mr. Snow hadn't been in favour of letting the rooms off. He could look after the house perfectly well, he said, when Cyril was away. Tenants—well, you never knew who they were, or what they might be up to.

As far as the Trimbles were concerned, Mr. Snow turned out to be right. Cyril did know something about them, of course. They were Midlanders who had come south from Birmingham and bought a tobacconists' and newsagents' business in the large town near which Cyril lived: they had been in lodgings till they answered his advertisement. Others had answered it too, there had been quite a number of applicants for Cyril's five rooms. But they all had something against them—children, dogs, unreasonable requirements—whereas the Trimbles had nothing against them. They were a sober, serious couple who minded their own business and gave no trouble: Mr. Snow admitted that. He even made friends with them, came down from his eyrie to sit with them, and accompanied them to the vilage local, where, so report said, they were making headway in the (for a foreigner) never easy task of making friends.

And how well Cyril had got on with them! When they met on the staircase, which was almost the only occasion when they did meet—what smiles and hand-shakings there were, what solicitous inquiries into each other's health and comfort! How often Cyril would ask if everything was to their liking, and how invariably they would answer that they couldn't possibly be better off than they were! Mr. Trimble was tall and thin and sallow; he wasn't prepossessing but had a nice smile that flickered across his face. She was fair and stout and dumpy, with big blue eyes that smiled continually, and a faint foreign accent: she might have been an Austrian Jewess.

For several months, then, all went well, and Cyril was so used to its going well, and to his own automatic reactions to the Trimbles' unfailing amiability when they met on the stairs, that he began to take not only their amiability but their presence for granted. So what was his amazement when one day, happening to mention them to Mr. Snow, he received the chilling answer:

'I haven't seen much of them lately.'

'Not seen much of them? I thought you saw a good deal of them.'

'At the start I did,' said Mr. Snow. 'But it often happens that things don't go on as they began—'

Cyril's heart sank.

'I hadn't noticed anything—'

'You will, sir, you can take my word for it.'

'Do you know what's wrong?' Cyril asked.

'I have an idea, sir, a very shrewd idea, but I shouldn't dream of telling you.'

'Oh, do tell me,' Cyril begged.

'No, sir, those things are best left in the minds of those who invented them.'

Cyril was not left long in doubt, however. When next he met the Trimbles on the stairs they did not return his greeting. Disappearing behind their door of partition they shut it none too gently. But the time after that they stood their ground, and Mr. Trimble said:

'I'd like a word with you, Mr. Hutchinson.'

Cyril noticed that contrary to custom, he was smiling but his wife was not. Resenting the man's tone, he said:

'I'm rather busy now. Will another time do?'

'I'm afraid it won't, Mr. Hutchinson. You see we're not standing for it.'

'I didn't ask you to stand,' said Cyril.

'Mr. Hutchinson, you're trying to evade the issue. I said we're not standing for it, we are giving notice. But first we want an explanation.'

'Yes, we want an explanation,' repeated his wife, with a set face.

'An explanation of what?' Cyril asked, mortified to feel that he was trembling.

'Don't try to evade the issue, Mr. Hutchinson,' put in Mrs. Trimble. 'We want an explanation of the interference.'

'The interference?' repeated Cyril. 'What sort of interference? Do you mean electrical interference? Are you speaking of your television set? I know the reception here is none too good.'

'Mr. Hutchinson, bluffing won't get you anywhere. We want your explanation before we report the matter to the police.'

'The police? What on earth do you mean?'

'Come, come, Mr. Hutchinson, you know quite well what we mean.'

The reiteration of his name infuriated Cyril.

'Unless you stop annoying me, Mr. Trimble *and* Mrs. Trimble,' he shouted, '*I'll* call the police and give you in charge for insulting language and behaviour. Now for the last time, what is this interference you complain of?'

Mr. Trimble's smile at last left his face, and he said sullenly:

'The interference with our things.'

'Interference with your things?' Like many mild men, when he lost his temper Cyril lost it thoroughly. 'Are you accusing me of some act of indecency? I wouldn't interfere with your things . . . not with a barge pole.'

He saw his anger had cowed them.

'All we know is,' the man said, 'someone has been in our apartments, moving things about, reading our letters, prying and spying. And who can it be but you? You've got the duplicate keys.'

Cyril drew a long breath.

'That settles it,' he said. 'I'll call the police.'

They both protested that this was the last thing they wanted; they even denied having mentioned the police at all. But Cyril was adamant. They had appealed to the police and they should have the police. Crestfallen, the couple shut the door on themselves, and Cyril retired to his study, fuming and shaking. Any declared enmity made him feel ill.

The village copper was an old friend of Cyril's and predisposed in his favour. All the same, he conducted his inquiry in an impartial manner. Mr. Snow was summoned, and the daily woman. Mr. Snow said that he had been in the Trimbles' sitting-room a few times, at their express invitation; he suggested he had never wanted to go. Asked if he had ever moved any of their things, he did not at first answer; then he said temperately, 'No, why should I? I've got my own things to look after.' The daily help was still more nonchalant. Yes, she had heard of the Trimbles and knew they occupied part of Mr. Hutchinson's house; when pressed she admitted she had passed the time of day with them, but that was all: she was a woman who kept herself to herself. 'It's the only way,' she added darkly. She didn't look at the Trimbles while she was speaking; she gave the impression that they were not there. Cyril could not emulate his retainers' lofty unconcern, but repeated his denials of any sort of interference in the Trimbles' quarters. He laughed nervously after saying this, it seemed so absurd that the ambiguities of language should again betray him into an impropriety; but the policeman did not notice. Asked if they had missed anything as a result of the interferences, the Trimbles admitted that they hadn't. The policeman shrugged his shoulders. Could he see the room where the alleged interferences occurred? They trooped down into the sitting-room, which was long, low and oval at the garden end. Furniture had been moved, said Mr. Trimble; this chair, for instance, had been there; and these letters—he pointed to them but didn't hand them round—had been taken from this drawer and put in that one. Ornaments had been moved and a table-lamp knocked over; but no damage had been done and nothing was missing. In that case, the policeman said, he could take no action; he hoped there would be no recurrence of the interferences; but if anything was stolen or damaged they must let him know.

Nothing was; and after the Trimbles had gone, taking their belongings with them, Mr. Snow gave it as his opinion that the whole thing had been a frame-up on their part, staged to cover the fact that they had found a better job elsewhere, and wanted to break their lease. The other possibility, that Mrs. Trimble had reached an age when women were liable to imagine interferences of various kinds, he discounted; besides, it was the man who brought the matter up. 'In my opinion, sir, you're well rid of them,' he said. 'I never did hold with having them here—it was different with the Gooches—at least they worked for you. And they never complained of interferences. You may be sure it was a put-up job.'

Cyril wasn't so sure. He felt he had been too hasty. The question of the interferences was not brought up again. After a period of cutting each other on the stairs, the Trimbles and he resumed relations—distant relations it is true, but such as permitted him to say goodbye to them with some show of goodwill. And he got the impression that they were sorry to go. But the whole episode left a bad taste in his mouth, of which the always unpleasant experience of having to dislike someone you have previously liked was only part.

So the five rooms were left tenantless, swept but not garnished. Cyril occasionally inspected them. A sort of compulsion, tingling with expectancy and dread, drew him towards them. Their very emptiness contained a sort of personality; he was aware of it the moment he unlocked the door: he felt he ought to apologize for intruding. The habit grew on him; the day seemed incomplete unless he had paid the rooms a visit. Sometimes he put this off until the evening when the summer twilight softened the impact of the glare from the bright curtainless windows on bare walls and uncarpeted floors; sometimes he left the inspection until bedtime, when he had to use a torch, for the Trimbles had taken with them all the detachable electric bulbs. Sneaking about on tiptoe he felt he was up to no good; passers-by, seeing the light flash from his torch, might think mischief was afoot and report it. The Dong with the Luminous Nose! But no, they wouldn't, for there were no passers-by: that side of the house was bounded by the river and the trees that bordered it: even the policeman couldn't see him. As time went on, one daily or nightly visit did not seem enough: he felt he must repeat his tour of inspection and maybe repeat it more than once, perhaps in his pyjamas, in case some aspect of the emptiness had escaped him. At such times he felt a heightened sense of being, as if he was in communication with something, and he would come away sweating and exhausted, as though from some nameless spiritual effort.

One day Mr. Snow said to him, 'Why don't you let me look round those empty rooms, sir, instead of you? I can do it last thing, when I lock up.' Cyril was startled: he had no idea that Mr. Snow had caught him at his little games. He thought quickly. Might this be a way out of his obsession—for such he recognized it to be? Would his subconscious mind, that throve on sacrifice, accept Mr. Snow's sacrifice of time and trouble as a substitute for his? At least let him try. 'Yes,' he said, 'that would be very kind of you, Mr. Snow. And would you come and tell me before you go to bed that everything's in order?'

Soon after eleven o'clock a knock came at his study door, and after the interval that elapsed before anyone entering the room could circumvent the screen that shielded his armchair from draughts, or other forms of surprise, the gardener stood before him. 'I have to report, sir, that all is present and correct,' he said, reminding Cyril that he had served in the army in the First World War—and with a little salute he was gone, almost before Cyril had had time to thank him.

Cyril struggled with himself, or rather with the part of him, the inward trouble-maker, that was so intent on upsetting his peace of mind. Was this the solution? How could he be sure that Mr. Snow had seen—all there was so see? Would he feel obliged to check up on the gardener's nocturnal investigations, which would almost certainly have been less thorough than his own? Would Mr. Snow have known exactly *what* to look for? The fact that Cyril himself did not know made the question no less urgent. And there was another question—ought he to let Mr. Snow take the *risk*?

His mind's unconscious use of italics brought Cyril to the

verge of realizing how absurd was his neurotic dilemma—a realization which had before now exorcized his sick fancies. It was all too silly! Of course there was no risk. Mr. Snow might be a year or two nearer seventy than he, Cyril, was; but he was hale and hearty, a match for any tenant, any imaginary tenant, he might encounter in those empty rooms. Besides, he had volunteered for this night-service; Cyril hadn't asked him to take it on.

Gradually the urgent sense of something left undone that would haunt his sleepless hours—perhaps make them sleepless—faded, and on that night, and for many subsequent nights, Cyril went to bed without misgivings. 'All present and correct!' *What* was present? It didn't matter, if what was present was correct.

Rarely did Cyril feel sleepy after dinner, but sometimes he did, and this was one of those times. It didn't mean he would sleep well at night, rather the opposite, so he tried to fight it off. Do what he would his head kept nodding and if he let it loll on the chair-back a host of scenes and impressions, unrelated to each other or to his present situation, flooded into it. Once or twice Mr. Snow, returning from his nightly round, had found him asleep, a thing Cyril much disliked—he hated being taken at a disadvantage, with an unprepared expression on his face that might reveal who knew what about his private thoughts. And this danger was real and imminent for eleven o'clock was drawing on; at any moment now he might expect the knock that heralded Mr. Snow's appearance.

At last it came, louder, he thought, than usual. Thankful for his wakefulness, he called out, 'Come in!' To his surprise, nothing happened. It was most unusual for Mr. Snow to need telling twice. 'Come in,' he called again and then he heard the door open, and footsteps behind the screen, and put on the smile of welcome he kept for Mr. Snow.

But it wasn't Mr. Snow who stood towering over him—it was a stranger, a huge man with a red, pear-shaped face, and eyes as black as the moustache which mounted guard over his unseen mouth. After a moment's silence, 'Good evening,' said the stranger. 'Good evening,' said Cyril, and rose uncertainly to his feet. 'You said come in, so I came in,' said the man. 'I hope I don't intrude?'

'Of course not,' Cyril answered. 'But . . . but . . .' He didn't know how to go on and added, 'Please sit down.' The stranger seated himself in the farthest away of the three chairs and Cyril sank back into his.

'I came to look for something, that's why I'm here,' the man said, 'and I thought perhaps you could help me to find it. I see the birds have flown.'

'If you mean the Trimbles—' began Cyril.

'I do mean them,' the stranger said. 'In their rooms was something of mine that I want back.'

'What is it?' Cyril asked.

'I'm not at liberty to say,' the stranger said.

'Then I'm afraid I can't help you,' Cyril said. 'They left some weeks ago and took all they had with them.'

The stranger nodded.

'But it may still be here,' he said. 'Don't you ever feel there's something here, waiting to be found?'

'If you would tell me what it was—'

'No, that I can't do,' said the man. 'But I'll tell you what I can do—I can take these rooms of yours that are standing empty, and then I may come across it. You let the rooms, don't you?'

'No,' said Cyril.

'You let them to the Trimbles.'

'Yes, and I wish I hadn't.'

'You'd find me a quiet tenant, Mr. . . . .'

'Hutchinson is the name.'

'You'd find me a quiet tenant, Mr. Hutchinson. You wouldn't hear me much or see me much. You'd know what I was doing—you wouldn't have to keep tabs on me—'

'I tell you I don't want to let the rooms,' said Cyril.

But the man steam-rollered on as if he hadn't spoken.

'There are the others, of course.'

'The others?'

'Yes, there are seven of us, but we could all squeeze in.'

'Haven't I told you I don't want to let the rooms?' cried Cyril in mounting exasperation.

'Yes, but hadn't you better think again, and take us in, since you can't keep us out?'

'Can't keep you out?' repeated Cyril, staring at him. 'You'll see if I can't keep you out!'

He jumped to his feet. The man rose too, huge, powerful, immovable, the heaviest single object in the room. But when Cyril threw himself on him he wasn't there—he had dissolved into a black mist, impalpable to Cyril's groping hands. When Cyril came to himself he was back in his chair, his mind awhirl with conflicting speculations. Who was he? Where was he? Had he fainted? Had he been asleep?

He glanced at the clock. Nearly half-past eleven. Why didn't Mr. Snow come? Had something happened to him? Ought Cyril to go in search of him? 'Mr. Snow! Mr. Snow!' No good calling him; whether he was upstairs, in his own rooms, or downstairs, in those other rooms, he could never hear, so many doors and staircases intervened.

If anything had happened to Mr. Snow it would be Cyril's fault for letting him take the risk, an elderly man armed only with a torch. Supposing he wasn't in the house at all, supposing he had seen something that upset him, and had wandered into the streets? Then Cyril would be quite alone in the house, at anybody's mercy.

So when the knock came, he didn't at once answer it, not

knowing who the visitor might be. And when it turned out to be Mr. Snow, with his thin Vandyck face and steady eyes, Cyril could hardly refrain from some demonstration of joy—shaking hands with him or even kissing him. Back to normal! Normal might be a dull-sounding word, but how blessed it was when applied to the temperature or the spirits! Down to normal, up to normal, dead normal.

'I didn't come before, sir,' Mr. Snow apologized, 'because I heard that you had company.'

'Company, Mr. Snow?'

'Yes, sir, I heard you talking to someone.'

Cyril was silent; then he said:

'You heard me talking to someone, but did you hear anyone talking to me?'

'I couldn't say, sir.' Mr. Snow's tone registered a slight affront. 'I heard your voice, sir, and then of course I didn't listen any longer. I thought someone had dropped in to call on you.'

'But wasn't the street door locked?'

'No, sir, nor the door downstairs, because I hadn't done my round yet. Actually, I came in from the garden through "their" door, you know.' The Trimbles were always 'they' to Mr. Snow.

'Did you see anyone in the garden?'

'Well, sir, I might have seen someone, some unauthorized person, I won't say that I didn't, but you know how dark it is, I couldn't be sure. I switched my torch on, because you can't be too careful, but I didn't see what you could call a person. Were you thinking it might have been your visitor, sir?'

'Yes—no—I—'

'Anyhow,' said Mr. Snow firmly, 'I'm glad to be able to report that all is now present and correct. Good night, sir.' Giving his little salute, Mr. Snow withdrew.

All absent and correct, yes; all present and incorrect, yes;

but present and correct, no: the two ideas were mutually exclusive. Conscientious as Mr. Snow undoubtedly was, sharp as his old eyes might be, certain things were outside his range of vision, if not beyond his hearing. He might not see what there was to see, and it wouldn't be fair, in future, to let him take the risk. Cyril waited till he was out of earshot, then took the torch he had left on the hall table, and with stealthy tread began to grope his way downstairs—an anonymous, questing figure, invisible behind his torch, his whereabouts unknown.

Was *he* the something his visitor had come to look for? Was he? Was he? He felt lost now; what would it feel like to be found?

Noughts and Crosses

FREDERICK CROSS had lost his diary and without it he was, in the face of the future, helpless. He relied on it absolutely. The mere act of writing in it left as little impression in his memory as if his memory had been the sands of the seashore. He had to have the book itself. 'Bring me my tablets!'

But no one in Smith's Hotel, where he was staying, could bring them, and retribution had come swiftly, for this very evening he was expecting some people to dinner and he didn't know who they were. He didn't know their names and wouldn't recognize their faces. He just remembered he had asked them for tonight.

It would have been very much worse, of course, if it had been the other way round—if he had been dining with them. That would have been a real settler. The only hope was that they would ring him up to confirm the engagement—a very slender hope. They still might, though it was now half-past seven, and dinner was at eight.

He remembered how the invitation had come about: it had come about, as invitations often do, at a cocktail-party. His host had led him up to Mr. Blank and said: 'I am sure you will have a lot to talk to each other about, Fred. Mr. Blank has just started as a publisher, and he is very much interested in the Jacobean Dramatists.'

Fred had written a book on the Jacobean Dramatists which no publisher had seen fit to take. With almost indecent haste he had invited Mr. Blank to dinner, and for good measure had included his wife in the invitation. Hardly had he got the words out, and given the publisher his address and the time for meeting, when they were swept away from each other. He had had no time to take in his interlocutor's appearance; not a single feature remained in his memory, and as for the wife, he never saw her, though he understood she was at the party.

However, in a few minutes the mystery would be solved. He had nothing to do but wait, and the hotel porter would announce his guests. To ensure that this should happen he lingered in his bedroom; the porter would then have to ring him up and notify him of the guests' arrival.

Punctually at eight o'clock the telephone bell rang and the porter's voice said: 'A lady and gentleman to see you, sir.' 'What is their name?' Fred asked, but disappointingly the porter had rung off.

The couple were standing in the lounge, the middle lounge, for there were three: one across the passage, one divided from the middle lounge by a wall of glass. Fred Cross went up to greet his guests.

'This is my wife, Mr. Cross,' the man said, introducing a rather florid-looking lady, whose face broke into a smile with many lateral wrinkles. The man was tall and dark and clean-shaven, it wasn't easy to place him; he didn't look especially like a publisher, but then what publisher does? He didn't look like anyone whom Fred remembered; but there was nothing remarkable in that: the party had been a blur of faces.

When they had sat down with their inevitable dry martinis and had exchanged a few platitudes about the weather (it was a coldish night in November) the man said:

'We are particularly pleased to see you, Mr. Cross, because there is a matter in which I think we could help each other. I daresay you know what it is.'

Fred was, on the whole, a man of direct speech and inclined

to come to the point straightaway; but he was used to the oblique approach of business men, and ready to adopt it.

'Well, yes,' he said, 'I rather think I do.' In his mind's eye he saw the typescript of his work on the Jacobean Dramatists, which the hands of many publishers' readers had dog-eared. At the risk of sounding facetious he added, with a smile:

'It's to do with something that happened a good while ago.'

'Yes, it is,' the man said. He did not smile, but his wife smiled brilliantly, showing her teeth.

'When we have talked it over,' said the man, 'perhaps you wouldn't mind coming round to our place, where you may find one or two more who are interested. Joe Cossage, for instance.' He looked at Fred Cross rather closely.

The name Joe Cossage conveyed nothing to Fred, but the field of Jacobean studies was a wide one, and he couldn't be expected to have heard of all the gleaners in it.

'I should be delighted,' he said, trying to conceal his eagerness. 'But shouldn't we have dinner first?'

'Dinner?' said the man, and if Fred hadn't been so engrossed in thinking about his book, he would have noticed the question mark and the time-lag before his guest said: 'Dinner would be a very good idea.'

'Of course, I haven't got the book with me,' Fred remarked.

'We didn't suppose you would have, did we, Wendy?' the man said to his wife who flashed her smile at his unsmiling face. 'But we should like to have a look at it, I can tell you, and so would Joe.'

'I mean, I haven't got it here,' said Fred, blushing for himself and his over-eagerness to sell his wares. 'As it happens—' he tried to make his voice sound casual—'as it happens I've got it upstairs.'

'Whew!' said the man, and something that might have been his soul, if he had one, seemed to appear in his face, so intense was his expression. 'Can we wait till after dinner, Wendy?'

'If Mr. Cross wants us to, I'm sure we can,' his wife said.

'Oh, yes, let's wait till afterwards,' said Fred, lightly. He regretted his unbusiness-like precipitancy, now that he saw that the others were just as anxious to see the book as he was to show it to them.

'As long as you don't change your mind about it,' said the man. 'We weren't sure you'd want us to see it, were we, Wendy?'

'Joe thought he'd come across with it,' his wife said, smiling.

'Well, a lot hangs on it, you see,' the man said, 'a lot hangs on it. That's why we weren't sure—'

'And a lot hangs on it for me, too,' Fred Cross interrupted.

The man glanced at him quickly. 'Yes, I suppose it does,' he said. 'That's why we thought persuasion might be necessary.'

Fred felt immensely flattered. Persuasion, indeed! If they only knew how he was longing to part with his treasure! But he mustn't let them know. He had already shown his hand too plainly.

'I won't be too unreasonable,' he said. 'I'll meet you as far as I can.'

The man seemed to notice his change of tone, for he said:

'We don't want just to look at it, you know. We want to *have* it.'

'Of course, of course,' Fred Cross said soothingly. 'After dinner we can talk about terms.'

'We'd better do that at our place,' the man said.

'Just as you like,' said Fred Cross, rather grandly. 'Now what about another round of drinks?'

They agreed. As Fred was going to the bar to give his order the porter came up to him and said: 'A lady and gentleman have just come and asked for you, sir.'

'Another lady and gentleman?'

'Yes, sir, there they are. They came a second ago, sir. I was just going to tell you.'

Fred followed the porter's eye. The couple were standing in the next lounge, with their backs to him, looking about them with the relaxed curiosity of people whose minds are comfortably on their dinners.

Oh, that damned diary! Here was another muddle. What was he to do? Five was an awkward number. How did he know the two couples would mix? And how could he introduce them to each other when he didn't know either of their names? Perhaps the porter could enlighten him.

'They didn't give a name, sir,' the porter said. 'They simply asked for you.'

Just as he feared! What an embarrassment to have to ask the two couples to introduce themselves to each other, and also to him! And who were the second couple, anyway? From a back view he didn't seem to know them, either. But better not look. He would have to act quickly. It would be a disaster, he now saw, if the second couple stayed, just as he was on the point of concluding a deal with these new publishers. For politeness' sake they would all have to talk about other things, and the opportunity might slip through his fingers, never to return. He *must* get rid of them.

To give himself a breathing space, he said to the porter:

'Perhaps another time you would ask visitors to give their names?'—but even while he saw the man's face stiffening under the rebuke he remembered that he might need his co-operation, that in fact he needed it now, and added quickly:

'Charlie, would you do this for me? Tell the lady and gentleman that I'm terribly sorry, but I've been taken ill, in fact I am in bed, and I can't give them dinner tonight. I shall be in the bar—just tell me if it's O.K.'

He crossed the bar (ill-omened phrase) and in a minute or two the porter informed him that the couple had gone. 'They said they were very sorry to hear you were ill, sir,' the man concluded, not altogether without malice.

'Oh, well.' Fred Cross sighed with relief, but he felt uncomfortable. He didn't like telling lies or getting other people to tell them for him; and he was superstitious enough to wonder whether saying he was ill might not make him ill, or bring him bad luck in some way.

When he rejoined his guests he seemed to have been away for hours, though in fact it was only a few minutes. The arrival of the drinks coincided with his apologies and smoothed over the interruption; but the conversational thread had snapped and it was only when dinner had been some time under way that they picked it up again. His guests seemed to fight shy of it, and Fred wondered if this was a policy they had agreed on between themselves, while he was out of hearing, with a view to lowering the advance they were prepared to pay on the book, or the royalty, or both.

'There are so many Smith's Hotels in London,' the woman was saying, with her bright automatic smile, 'almost as many as there are Smith's bookshops. We weren't quite sure which yours was.'

'Joe told us it would be this one,' said her husband, glancing at Fred.

Again Fred wondered who this Joe might be, who seemed so conversant with his whereabouts. But it wasn't by any means the first time that a stranger to him had furnished a third party with his address. More people know Tom Fool than Tom Fool knows. But he had every reason to be grateful to Joe, whoever he was.

'Yes, there are a lot of Smith's Hotels,' he agreed. 'But,' he added humorously, 'I think this is the chief one. And for that matter'—the thought struck him suddenly—'there are quite a lot of Frederick Crosses. It's a common name. I know another myself.'

'Yes, Joe thought there might be another,' said the man, 'but as it turned out he was wrong.'

'I'm glad he was,' said Fred. 'I can't think of another Fred Cross who has to do with books. And this hotel is quite a haunt of literary men.'

'Of men with books to sell?' said his guest, lowering one eyelid into what, if it had been more mirthful, might have been a wink.

'Yes, men with books to sell,' said Fred, delighted to have got back to books at last. 'And men who have sold them too, of course. Now as for mine—'

'We want to see the book first, you know, we want to know what's in it, don't we, Wendy?'

'Oh, well, you shall,' said Fred, cautious now in his turn, 'that is if you're really interested, as you seem to be.' If they were on their guard, so would he be on his. He would whet their curiosity with hints. 'I could give you a bit—'

'All in good time,' the man said hurriedly. 'All in good time, but a list is what we want.'

'A list of names, I mean,' Fred went on, 'my authorities— my colleagues, I suppose I could call them since I'm a bit of an authority myself—a bibliography, you know. And I've done quite a lot of research, too. I've dug about in all sorts of places that most people don't know about, besides London and Oxford and Cambridge. Oh, I've unearthed some interesting facts—facts, let me tell you, not just hypotheses. You'd be surprised how much I've learnt.'

The husband and wife listened in silence; then the man said, sipping his wine, 'It's facts we're chiefly interested in, facts and names. You said you went to Cambridge?'

'Oh, yes, I did quite a lot of work in Cambridge. In Cambridge it's comparatively simple—people are ready to tell you what they know.'

'Did you come across Ben Jonson in Cambridge?' the man asked, lowering his voice.

Fred Cross laughed.

G

'Oh, yes, of course I did.'

'And Jack Webster?'

'I expect you mean John Webster,' Fred corrected him.

'I daresay he's called John sometimes,' said the man.

'Of course I know him,' Fred said. 'He's my favourite. But I didn't find out much about him.'

'Your favourite, is he?' the man said, disagreeably. 'Well, there's no accounting for tastes. And who else did you dig up? Did you dig up Dick Skipton?'

This name was strange to Fred. Was Dick Skipton a dramatist, or a critic, or a scholar—someone he ought to have heard of? He didn't want to admit a gap in his omniscience, they would think the worse of him if he did, so he said casually, taking a chance, and hoping that Dick Skipton wasn't dead, 'If I didn't meet him I heard a lot about him.'

'You seem to be well in with the whole bunch,' observed the man in a neutral voice, and his wife gave her quick smile, which seemed at the moment oddly out of place.

'Well, it's my job to be,' said Fred Cross, modestly. 'I've spent several years, you know, trailing them, tracking them down. I flatter myself that I know as much about them as anyone does. I believe that you are interested in them, too. If you care to ask me a question about any of them, sir, I should be only too glad to answer it if I can.'

Rather to Fred's surprise, his guest didn't take up the challenge. Instead he said, yawning into his wife's smile:

'I'm ready to take your word for it.'

Fred thought that this was carrying the pose of indifference rather far. 'It's been a labour of love, you know,' he said. And when they looked rather rudely incredulous, he added: 'It may be morbid of me, but I like the company of all those thugs and assassins.'

'You're welcome to them,' the man said rather grimly. 'But the main thing is, you've got their dossiers.'

'Oh yes, I have,' Fred said. 'But I'm sorry you don't like them. They did things so picturesquely. "Enter executioners with coffin, cords and a bell." The killers of today are ... well ... more prosaic.'

'I'll say they are,' said his guest, with a sudden lapse into Americanese. 'I'll say they are. Now, Wendy, we must go and make up our faces, and then we'll take Mr. Cross on to our place. It's not too early for you, is it, Mr. Cross? We've got the car outside.'

'No, indeed,' said Fred. He felt the meal was being terminated rather abruptly; but he was as anxious as his guests seemed to be to get down to business.

Left alone, he sat for a moment at the table, thinking. No doubt the pair, besides powdering their noses, wanted to say a word to each other in private about terms. While they were doing that he would go upstairs and fetch the book. Even his rather shabby bedroom wore a cheerful air, such was his elation, and when he took the typescript out of his suitcase, instead of greeting him with the leaden look of a child that has never managed to make good—the look that only an oft-rejected typescript can give—it seemed to say: 'Your faith in me has been justified after all.' I'll wrap it up, he thought, handling it affectionately; it won't matter if I keep them waiting, it'll make them the more eager. How often had he done up this selfsame parcel; even the brown paper had been used before. But this would be its last outward journey until it returned to him with his proofs.

The book under his arm, he walked downstairs, scorning the lift. As he was crossing the middle lounge—always some Rubicon for a Cross to cross—he heard his name called. Not a good sign had the voice been imaginary, but this time it was real, as real at any rate as the loudspeaker's voice, which penetrated to the very nerve-centres. 'Mr. Whiston, please. A telephone call for Mr. Whiston, please. Mr. Fred Cross would

like to speak to Mr. Whiston. Mr. Fred Cross calling Mr.
Whiston, please.'

The hotel seemed to echo with it. Of all the coincidences on
this evening of coincidences, this was the one that surprised
Fred Cross the least. Experience had taught him that there
were other Fred Crosses in the world besides himself. It was a
lesson in humility which he had thoroughly learnt. Sometimes
it vaguely depressed him that he had to share his name with so
many other men but tonight he was proof against depression;
he was morally certain that his 'Jacobean Dramatists' was in
the bag (what bag? whose bag? A bag unknown to Brewer's
Phrase and Fable).

As the message was being repeated, the porter said to him:

'Your guests are waiting for you in the car, sir.'

He sat on the back seat with the publisher's wife, and didn't
notice much where they were going, so occupied was he in
trying to keep up a conversation with her invisible but (he felt
sure) existent smile. True to his resolution, he gave away as
little as he could, and she was just as unforthcoming. Their
conversation, like an iceberg, trailed unmeasured depths beneath it. Childishly, Fred found this mystification rather fun.

London spreads out a long way in all directions; when at last
Fred felt he could take a rest from social effort and look about
him he didn't know where he was, but the street lamps were
fewer than they had been, and the houses farther apart. A
minute or two later the man said: 'This is us,' and drew up
at the kerb.

The 'place' he had been taken to was much less grand than
the size of the car suggested that it would be: it was in fact a
bed-sitting-room in a semi-detached house. Many people lived
like that nowadays, but they generally made the bed, or got it
made, before the evening. As though aware of his thought the
woman said:

'Sorry the room's in such a mess, but we had to make an early start this morning. What about some whisky, Bill?'

'In there,' the man said briefly, indicating a small cupboard which, when opened, was seen to house a surprising number of objects meant for a variety of uses: but drinking was one of them.

When the gas-fire had been lit the room seemed more habitable, as well as warmer. Fred and his hostess occupied the armchairs on each side of it; the man cleared a space among the bedclothes and sat down on the bed.

'Joe's not here,' he said.

'He may be on some job,' said Wendy.

'Well, good luck to him and good luck to the book,' he said.

'To the book!' he said, and raised his glass. They all drank to it and Fred was suddenly aware of the parcel under his arm. Self-consciously but proudly he began to fumble with the string. This was his moment.

'Some book!' the man said, watching him.

Fred agreed. 'It took me—' he broke off, remembering he had told them before how long the book had taken him to write—remembering, too, that publishers are not necessarily impressed by the extent of an author's industry. 'Well, you know how long it took me,' he substituted. 'Time wasn't an object: accuracy was what I aimed at.'

They both nodded, and out the typescript came. It had at once, for his eyes, the too bulky, too ponderous look of a literary work, however slender, that has always missed its market. Printed in the middle was the title, its worn, faded ink almost indecipherable against the pale blue of the folder, and in the bottom right-hand corner Fred's name, and his address, which seemed at the moment very far away.

The man took the book from him. 'I wasn't expecting a big book like this,' he said, 'I must put on my glasses.' The horn-rimmed spectacles transformed his face and for the first time he looked like a man who might be interested in books. He turned the pages. 'Middleton, Marston, haven't heard of them. Oh, here's Ben Jonson. Where's the list you spoke of?'

'You'll find it at the end,' said Fred.

The man began to read the names out, and then stopped. 'Strikes me there's some mistake here,' he said. 'Somebody's been having a game,' he repeated giving the innocent phrase an unpleasant sound. 'A game with us, it looks like. Somebody has. What do you make of it, Wendy?'

He handed his wife, if wife she was, the book: the pages turned rapidly under her reddened nails.

'I can't make head or tail of it,' she said. 'It might be some-body's idea of a joke. . . . Perhaps this gentleman will explain.'

Fred cleared his throat.

'It's my book,' he said, with such dignity as he could muster, but with a fluttering at his midriff. 'My book on the Jacobean Dramatists. I thought you were interested in it. . . . I was told you were.'

'Who told you?' the man asked.

It was only when he couldn't remember his informant's name—a name he knew as well as his own—that Fred realized he was frightened.

'But you are publishers, aren't you?' he asked.

For a moment it seemed just rude that neither of them answered; then it seemed strange, with the strangeness of their faces, the strangeness of the room, and the strangeness of his being there at all.

'I thought—' he began.

'You thought a good deal, didn't you?' said the man. 'It's our turn to think now. Someone, as the poet said, has blun-dered. Someone will be for it, I suppose.'

The repetition of the word 'someone' began to get on Fred Cross's nerves.

'If you're not interested,' he said, half-rising, 'I'll take the book away.'

'Sit down, sit down,' the man said, patting the air above Fred's head. 'We *are* interested, and we don't want you to go away, not yet. We haven't quite done with you, as the saying is. Now as for this book—'

'It's quite simple,' said Fred, trembling. 'I see you're not interested in it. I'll take it away.'

'It isn't so simple as that,' the man said. 'Someone has found out something that someone has got to forget—or there may be trouble, and we don't want any trouble, do we?'

'No,' said Fred mechanically.

'I'm not mentioning names,' the man went on, 'it's better not to mention names, we haven't mentioned names, have we?'

'You know my name,' Fred said.

'Yes, but we're not interested in your name. It's our names that matter. She's Wendy and I'm Bill—those are our names. You can call us by them, if you like.'

Fred Cross had never felt less inclined to be on Christian-name terms with anyone.

'And you might want to write to us,' Bill went on. 'You might want to send us a Christmas card, for instance.'

'I don't think I shall,' Fred said.

'You never know,' Bill said. 'Now here's an envelope.' He fetched one, slightly soiled, from a heap of litter on the table. 'Have you a pen?'

Using the typescript as a desk, Fred set himself to write; his hand was shaking.

'Mr. and Mrs.—' he wrote, and stopped. Then he remembered: Whiston, of course. 'Mr. Whiston, please. A telephone call for Mr. Whiston, please.' But his hand was shaking too much. To gain time he raised it from the envelope and said:

'But you haven't told me your name.'

'Didn't we tell you?' the man asked. 'It was very careless of us. Are you sure we didn't?'

'Quite sure,' said Fred.

'What an extraordinary thing. We didn't tell you our name, or our address, or anything?'

'Nothing at all,' said Fred.

'Could you find your way here, if you wanted to pay us another visit?'

Suddenly Fred wondered if he could frighten them, and rashly said:

'I think I could.'

'Oh, you think you could? Well, just to make it easier for you, here's our name and the address,' Bill said, standing behind him. 'Take it down.'

Fred bent his head and set himself to write.

'Allbright,' said the dictating voice.

'Mr. and Mrs. Allbright, Flat C, 19 Lavender Avenue, S.W.17. Got that?'

Fred did get it, but he couldn't say so, for his head was lying on the typescript, and he was unconscious. When he came to he was in hospital. A policeman had found him stretched on the pavement in a deserted street. Almost his first inquiry was for his precious typescript, and almost the first action when he left the hospital was to get in touch with the man whom he had turned so inhospitably from the door. All the newspapers had reported his misadventure, and none of them failed to observe that the typescript had bloodstains on it. At last it was in the news, and this may have turned the scale in Fred's favour; at any rate the publisher accepted it.

Yet more publicity followed. The name of Allbright conveyed nothing to the police, but the name Whiston did.

'You were lucky you didn't let on you knew it,' the police told Fred, 'or you would have got a bigger bashing than the one you did get.' They had more serious charges against William Whiston than the assault upon Fred Cross, but that was one charge. Another Fred Cross soon figured in the proceedings, a much more sensational one; but he did not altogether steal the limelight from our hero, for the newspapers dared not mention him and his black doings without making it quite clear that he must not be confused with another Fred Cross, the well-known author, whose long-awaited work on the Jacobean Dramatists was soon to be given to the world. But one important piece of evidence in the case, a small black notebook containing a list of the names of a gang against whom William Whiston had a grudge, was never submitted to a publisher.

The Pylon

The trees sloping inwards, and the hedge bounding the field beyond, made a triangle of green in which the pylon stood. Beyond it, fields again and then the railway embankment. Beyond the embankment more hedges making transverse lines, and then the roofs of houses bowered in trees, sloping up to the wooded hill-crest, outlined against the sky. But that was a mile, perhaps, two miles away; whereas the pylon—

There was general rejoicing when the pylon disappeared: Mummy was glad, Daddy was glad, Victor was glad and Susan was glad. The morning when it happened they all crowded to the window as if they had never seen the view before. Nor had they—the view without the pylon. Ever since they came to the house ten years ago it had been there—an eyesore, a grievance. 'It would be such a lovely view,' they used to say to visitors, 'if it wasn't for the pylon!'

The pylon used to stand between two trees, a fir-tree and a copper beech, directly in front of the window, just beyond the garden. Instead of concealing it, they framed it. Every so often Victor, the optimist, now sixteen, would say, 'Daddy, I'm sure those branches are coming closer together! Next year, you'll see, they'll hide it!' And his father would reply, as like as not, 'They're not growing any nearer—they're growing farther apart! Fir-trees and beech-trees don't agree, you know!'

There it stood, between the trees, rearing its slender tapering height against the wooded hillside, the line of which it mad-

deningly broke, topping with its incongruous yard-arm the
ancient earth-work that crowned the hill.

Now it was gone, and in its place they saw the trees that it
had hidden and, more especially, two Lombardy poplars growing so close together that if you walked a little distance, either
way, they looked like one.

And Laurie, the youngest of the family, too, was glad at first,
or thought he was. When he heard his parents saying to
visitors, 'Isn't it wonderful, the pylon's gone!' he would
echo, in a grown-up manner ill-suited to his eleven years,
'Yes, isn't it wonderful?' Not that he disliked the pylon on
aesthetic grounds, but he thought it was the proper thing to
say.

But whereas their grievance against the pylon had been
vocal for many years, their gratitude for its departure was comparatively short-lived. They would still say, 'How marvellous
without the pylon!' but they didn't really feel it, and after a
month or two they didn't even say it, taking their deliverance
for granted, just as when an aching tooth is pulled out, one
soon ceases to bless the painless cavity.

With Laurie, however, it was otherwise. Being outwardly a
conformer—indeed a rather zealous conformer—he had joined
in the delight his elders showed over the pylon's downfall. He
tried to gloat over the square patch of concrete, marking its
site, which the demolition squad hadn't bothered to clear
away. But when he stood in front of the window, whichever
window it might be—for having a southern aspect, most of
the windows of the house had once looked on the pylon—and
set himself to gloat, sometimes he would find his eyes straying,
even shying away from, the remnant of its ruin. To the others
the pylon had been an eyesore and a grievance; to him it was
a landmark and a friend. How tall and proud it used to be—
one hundred and seventeen feet high—the tallest object in the
neighbourhood—taller than the hill itself, he liked to think,

though his mind told him that its superior height was only a trick of the perspective.

From surveying the pylon-less gap with a lack-lustre eye it was a short step to trying to imagine it with the pylon there. And then Laurie realized that something had gone out of his life—some standard, was it, by which he had measured himself? No, not exactly that, nor only that. The pylon had symbolized his coming stature, his ambitions for himself as an adult. One day his short, plump body would shoot upwards, tall and straight as the pylon was; one day his mind, that was so dense in some ways, and so full of darkness, would fine down to an aery structure that let the light in everywhere and hardly cast a shadow. He would be the bearer of an electric current, thousands of volts strong, bringing light and power to countless homes.

The pylon, then, had served him as a symbol of angelic strength. But in other moods it stood for something different, this grey-white skeleton. In meaner moods, rebellious moods, destructive moods, he had but to look at it to realize how remote it was from everything that grew, that took its nourishment from the earth and was conditioned by this common limitation. It was self-sufficient, it owed nothing to anyone. The pylon stood four-square upon the ground, but did not draw its sustenance from the ground. It was apart from Nature; the wind might blow on it, the rain might beat on it, the snow might fall on it, frost might bite it, drought might try to parch it, but it was immune, proof against the elements: even lightning could not touch it, for was it not itself in league with lightning?

And so he, Laurie, in those moods when nothing favoured him, when everyone's hand was against him and his hand against theirs, insulated by the flawless circle of himself, he, too, enjoyed the pylon's immunity, its power to be itself. Whatever stresses might be brought to bear on it, it didn't care, nor, looking at it, did he, Laurie, care.

All that was over now; his companion was gone; and Laurie-the-pylon was no more.

Deprived of his second self he shrank, his imaginative life dwindled, and with it his other budding interests. An east-wind blight descended on his mind, dulling his vision, delaying his reactions. If he was spoken to, he didn't always hear, and if he heard he didn't always answer. 'But you don't *listen*!' Susan would chide him, in exasperation, and his brother, who went to the same day-school, would defend him: 'You see, he's so tiny, his ears haven't grown yet! They're really little baby's ears!' Then Laurie would lunge out at him, and in the scuffle regain the sense of immediate contact with reality that he had lost.

His mother and father, oddly enough, took longer to notice the change in him, for he had always been more talked against than talking. In fact they might never have noticed it but for his end-of-term reports. These made them think, and one, from Laurie's form-master, made them quite indignant.

'I wonder what's come over the boy,' his father said, knitting his heavy brows and tapping his finger-tips against his teeth. 'He used to be the clever one. Not quick and sharp like Victor, but thoughtful and original.'

'I expect he's going through a phase,' his wife said, placidly.

'Phase, indeed! He isn't old enough for phases.'

'You'd better speak to him, but if you do, be careful, darling. You know how sensitive he is.'

'Sensitive my foot! I'm much more sensitive than he is. You ought to warn *him* to be careful.'

'I only meant we don't want anything to do with Oedipus,' his wife said.

'You shouldn't spoil him, then. You should be much nastier to him than you are. I've more reason to worry about Oedipus than you have. Laurie might marry you, O.K., but he would murder me. It's *I* who am to be pitied. No one ever

pities fathers. No one ever pities Oedipus's father, whom
Oedipus bumped off. I think I shall expose Laurie on Mount
Cithaeron, having first stuck the toasting-fork through his toes.'

All the same, he put off 'speaking' to Laurie as long as he
could, and when the time came he approached the subject
warily.

'Well, old man,' he said, when he had got Laurie alone,
'take a pew and tell me how you fared last term.'

Deliberately he seated himself at some distance, for fear the
nearness of his large strong body might arouse the wrong kind
of response and inflict a Freudian bruise.

'Well,' echoed Laurie, heavily, 'I didn't do very well, I'm
afraid.'

'You're growing too fast, that's the trouble,' said his father.
'It takes it out of you.'

'I only grew an eighth of an inch last term. They measured
me,' Laurie added, almost as mournfully as if the measuring
had been for his coffin.

Drat the boy, his father thought. He won't use the loop-
holes that I offer him.

He pulled at his moustache which, unlike the bronze hair
greying on his head, had kept its golden colour. Proud of its
ability to keep its ends up unaided, he wore it rather long, a
golden bow arched across his mouth and reaching to the
wrinkles where his smile began. Tugging it was a counter-
irritant to emotional unease. But was such an adult, masculine
gesture quite suitable in front of a small boy?

'How do you account for it, then?' he asked, at last.

'Account for what, Daddy?' But Laurie knew.

'Well, for your reports not being so good as they sometimes
are.'

Laurie's face fell.

'Oh, weren't they good?'

'Not all that good. Mr. Sheepshanks—' he stopped.

'What did he say?' The question seemed to be forced out of Laurie.

Mr. Sheepshanks had said that Laurie's work was 'disappointing'. How mitigate that adjective to a sensitive ear?

'He said you hadn't quite come up to scratch.'

'I never was much good at maths,' said Laurie, as though he had had a lifetime's experience of them.

'No, they were never your strong suit ... And Mr. Smallbones—'

Laurie clasped his hands and waited.

Mr. Smallbones had said, 'Seems to have lost his wish to learn.' Well, so have I, his father thought, but I shouldn't want to be told so.

'He said ... well, that Latin didn't come easily to you. It didn't to me, for that matter.'

'It's the irregular verbs.'

'I know, they are the devil. Why should anyone want to learn what is irregular? Most people don't need to learn it.' He smiled experimentally at Laurie, who didn't smile back. He unclasped his hands and asked wretchedly, but with a slight lift of hopefulness in his voice:

'What did Mr. Armstrong say?'

Mr. Armstrong was Laurie's form-master, and it was his cruel verdict that had rankled most with Laurie's parents. It couldn't be true! It had seemed a reflection on them too, a slur on their powers of parenthood, a genetic smear, a bad report on *them*. And it was indignation at this personal affront, as well as despair of finding further euphemisms, that made him blurt out Mr. Armstrong's words.

'He said you were dull but deserving.'

Laurie's head wobbled on his too-plump neck and his face began to crinkle. Appalled, his father ran across to him and touched him on the shoulder, pressing harder than he knew with his big hand. 'Don't worry, old chap,' he said, 'don't worry. When I was your age I had terrible reports, much worse than yours are. You've spoilt us, that's what it is, by always having had such smashing ones. But now I've got some good news for you, so cheer up!'

Laurie raised his tear-stained face open-eyed to his father's and set himself to listen. His father moved away from him and, drawing himself up to give the fullest effect to his announcement, said:

'It doesn't matter so much what these under-masters say, it's what the *Head*master says that counts. Now the *Head*master says—'

Suddenly he forgot what the Headmaster had said, although he remembered that some parts of the report had best not be repeated. Reluctantly, for he meant to keep the incriminating document hidden, and believed he had its contents by heart, he pulled it out of his breast-pocket, ran his eyes over it, and began rather lamely:

'Mr. Stackpole says, hm . . . hm . . . hm—just a few general remarks, and then: "Conduct excellent". "Conduct excellent",' he repeated. 'You've never had that said of you before. It's worth all the others put together. I can't tell you how pleased and proud I am.'

He paused for the electrifying effect, but it didn't come. Instead, Laurie's face again began to pucker. For a moment he was speechless, fighting with his sobs; then he burst out miserably:

'But *anyone* can be good!'

Trying to comfort him, his father assured him that this wasn't true: very, very few people could be good, even he, Laurie's own father, couldn't, and those who could were worth their weight in gold. After a time he thought that he was making headway: Laurie's sobs ceased, he seemed to be listening and at last he said:

'Daddy, do you think they'll ever build the pylon up again?'

His father stared.

'Good lord, I hope not! Why, do you want them to?'

Laurie shook his head as if he meant to shake it off.

'Oh, no, no, no. Of course not. It's an eyesore. But I just thought they might.'

That night Laurie dreamed that he had got his wish. There stood the pylon: much as he remembered it, but bigger and taller. At least that was his impression, but as it was night in his dream he couldn't see very well. But he knew that he had regained his interest in life, and knew what he must do to prove it to himself and others. If he did this, a good report was waiting for him. But first he must get out of bed and put on his dressing-gown which lay across the chair, and go downstairs, silently of course, for if they were about they would hear and stop him. Sometimes, when he was sleepless, he would go out on to the landing and lean over the banisters and call out: 'I can't get to sleep!' and then they would put him to sleep in the spare-room bed, where later his father would join him. But long before his father came up he would be asleep, asleep as soon as his head touched the pillow, such an assurance of security did the promise of his father's presence bring.

And now if they heard him moving about he would just say that he couldn't get to sleep, and put off his visit to the pylon to another night. Oh, how clever he was! It was the return of the pylon into his life that made him clever.

Nobody heard him; they had gone to bed. The house was in darkness, but if he was a burglar he wouldn't mind about that: he would be glad; and Laurie-the-burglar was glad, too, as he tiptoed downstairs in his felt-soled slippers.

But the door—could he unlock it? Yes, the catch yielded to

his touch as it would have to a real burglar's, and he remembered not to shut it, for he must be able to get in again.

He went round to the front of the house. Now the pylon was in full view: its tapering criss-cross shape indistinct against the hill-side, as if someone had drawn it in ink on carbon paper with a ruler; but where it rose above the hill—and it soared much higher than it used to—it was so clear against the sky that you could see every detail—including the exciting cross-piece, just below the summit, that Laurie used to think of as its moustache.

With beating heart and tingling nerves he hastened towards it, through the garden gate and out into the field, feeling it impending over him long before he reached it, before he could even properly see where its four great legs were clamped into the concrete. Now he was almost under it, and what was this? Something grinning at him just above his head, with underneath the words: 'Danger de Mort'. Abroad all pylons had them. He hadn't needed to ask his father what the skull and crossbones meant; he hadn't needed to ask what 'danger de mort' meant: 'Your French is coming on!' his father said. In England pylons didn't bear this warning; the English were cleverer than the French—they knew without being told. In England pylons were not dangerous: could this be a French one?

It was a warm night but Laurie shivered and drew his dressing-gown more closely round him. But if there was danger of death, all the more reason to go on, to go up, to be one with the steel girders and the airs that played around them. But not in a dressing-gown, not in bedroom slippers, not in pyjamas, even! Not only because you couldn't climb in them, but because in them you couldn't feel the cold touch of the steel upon the flesh. It would be a kind of cheating: you wouldn't win the good report, perhaps, which depended, didn't it? on doing things the hardest way.

Lest anyone should steal his night attire Laurie hid it under a low bush close by the monster's base. Clever Laurie, up to every dodge! English pylons had steps—iron bolts like teeth sticking out six inches from two of the four great supporting girders, and reaching to the top, making the climb easy. But this one hadn't, so it must be a French pylon. He would have to climb the face of it, clinging to the spars as best he could, for the pylon was an empty shell until almost the top, where a network of struts and stays, like a bird's nest in a chimney, would give a better foot-hold.

When he had started he dared not look down to see if his clothes were still there, because climbers mustn't look down, it might make them giddy. Look up! Look up! The climbing wasn't as difficult as he thought it would be, because at the point where the girders met, to form an X like a gigantic kiss in steel, there was a horizontal crossbar on which he could stand and get his breath before the next attempt. All the same, it hurt; it hurt straddling the girders and it hurt holding them, for they were square, not rounded as he thought they would be, and sometimes they cut into him.

That was one thing he hadn't reckoned with; another was the cold. Down on the ground it had been quite warm; even the grass felt warm when he took his slippers off. But now the cold was like a pain: sometimes it seemed a separate pain, sometimes it mingled with the pain from his grazed and aching limbs.

How much farther had he to go? He looked up—always he must look up—and saw the pylon stretching funnel-wise above him, tapering, tapering, until, when he reached the bird's nest, it would scrape against his sides. Then he might not be able to go on; he might get wedged between the narrowing girders, like a sheep that has stuck its head through a fence and can't move either way.

And if he reached the top and clung to the yard-arm, which

was his aim, what then? What proof would he have to show them he had made the ascent? When his schoolfellows did a daring climb, they left something behind to show they had; the one who climbed the church-spire, clinging to the crockets, had left his cap on the weathercock; it had been there for days and people craned their necks at it. Laurie had nothing to leave.

And what had happened to him, this boy? What sort of report did he get? He had been expelled—that was the report he got. It had all happened many years ago, long before Laurie was born: but people still talked of it, the schoolboy's feat, and said it was a shame he'd been expelled. He should have been applauded as a hero, and the school given a whole holiday. Perhaps it was just as well for Laurie that he had nothing to leave, except some of his blood—for he was bleeding now— which wouldn't be visible from below. But they would believe him, wouldn't they, when he told them he had scaled the pylon? They would believe him, and make out his report accordingly? Would they say, 'Jenkins minor has proved himself a brave boy, he has shown conspicuous gallantry and devotion to duty, in that he has climbed the pylon which no boy of his age has ever climbed before, and in commemoration of this feat the school will be granted a whole holiday'?

Or would they say: 'Jenkins minor has been a very naughty boy. By climbing the pylon he has disgraced himself and the whole school. He will be publicly expelled in the school yard, and the school will forfeit all half-holidays for the rest of term'?

Well, let them say that if they wouldn't say the other! At any rate he would have made his mark.

Soon he was too tired to argue with himself: too tired and too frightened. For the pylon had begun to sway. He had expected this, of course. Being elastic the pylon would have to sway, and be all the safer because it swayed. But it shouldn't sway as much as this, leaning over first to one side, then to the other, then dipping in a kind of circle, so that instead of seeing its central point when he looked up, the point where all its spars converged, the point where his desires converged, the point which meant fulfilment, he saw reeling stretches of the sky, stars flashing past him, the earth itself rushing up to meet him. . . .

He woke and as he woke, before he had time to put a hand out, he was violently sick.

'I can't think what it can be,' his mother said. 'He can't have eaten anything that disagreed with him; he ate the same as we did. You didn't *say* anything to upset him, did you, Roger?'

'I told him about the reports,' her husband said. 'You asked me to, you know. I did it as tactfully as I could. I couldn't exactly congratulate him on them, except on his good conduct, which he didn't seem to like. Yes, I remember now, he *was* upset: I did my best to calm him down and thought I'd succeeded. I hope the poor boy isn't going crackers—we've never had anything like that in *my* family.'

'He's highly-strung, that's all, and your presence, Roger, is a bit overpowering. I know you don't mean it to be, but if I was a little boy—'

'Thank goodness you aren't.'

'I might be frightened of you.'

'How can he be frightened of me, when he wants to sleep with me?'

'I'm often frightened of you,' said his wife, 'but still I want to sleep with you.'

'This is getting us into deep waters,' Roger said, stretching himself luxuriously. 'But you won't be able to sleep with me tonight, my dear, because you've arranged for me to sleep with Laurie.'

'Yes, he's in the spare-room bed.'

'He'll never find another father as accommodating as I am.'

'Oh, I don't know.'

'At any rate I hope there won't be any repetition of the incident—the upshot, the fall-out, or whatever you call it.'

'I'm sure not, he was fast asleep when I left him. But you know, Roger, he *was* a bit light-headed—he kept muttering something about the pylon, very fast in that indistinct way children talk when they're ill and half-asleep—'

'I hope he doesn't take *me* for the pylon.'

'Oh dear, how silly you are. But what I mean is, if he wakes up and mentions the wretched thing, because it seems to be on his mind, just say—'

'What shall I say?'

'Say that it's dead and buried, or cremated, or on the scrap-heap, or whatever happens to pylons that have outlived their usefulness. Say that it's nothing to be afraid of, because it *doesn't exist*, and if it did—'

'Well?'

'If it did, which it doesn't, it's still nothing to be afraid of, because men made it and men have taken it down, taken it to pieces. It's not like Nature, there whether we want it or not; it's like the things he makes with his Meccano. From what I gathered he seemed to think it could have a kind of independent existence, go on existing like a ghost and somehow hurt him. He reads this science fiction and doen't distinguish very well between fiction and fact—children don't.'

'All right, all right,' said Roger. 'Don't worry, Anne. I shall have the situation well in hand. I shall say, if he wakes up, which please God he won't, "Now, Laurie, just pretend the pylon is me"—or I, to be grammatical. That will re-route his one-track mind, and turn it in a different direction.'

Anne thought a moment.

'I'm not sure that I should say that,' she said. 'If he asks you, hold on to the pylon being *artificial*, something that man has made and can unmake, and that's all there is to it.'

'Very well, dear wife,' said Roger, and they parted for the night.

Laurie was lying, cheeks flushed and breathing quickly, on the extreme edge of the bed, as he always did to give his father room. Gingerly Roger stole in beside him, and laid his long, heavy body between the sheets. Lights out! He slept late, for his wife wouldn't have them called, and woke up wondering if Laurie was awake.

He wasn't; his face was much less flushed and his breathing normal.

I'll stay in bed till he wakes up, his father thought. He may have something to say to me.

At length the boy began to stir; consciousness returned to him by slow stages, and deliciously, as it does in youth, down gladsome glades of physical well-being. Sighs, grunts and other inarticulate sounds escaped from him, and then he flung his arm out and hit his father full across the mouth.

'Hi, there, I'm not a punching-bag!'

Laurie woke up and gave his father a rueful, sheepish smile.

'Well, say good morning to me.'

'Good morning, Daddy.'

'Now I've got to get up. You, lazybones, can stay in bed if you like.'

'Why, Daddy?'

'Because you weren't too well last night. Your mother gave a poor report of you.' He paused, regretting the word, and added hastily, 'That's why you're here.'

Laurie's face changed, and all the happiness went out of it.

'Because I had a bad report?'

'No, silly, because you weren't well. You were sick, don't you remember? In other words, you vomited.'

Laurie's face lay rigid on the pillow: the shadow of fear appeared behind his eyes.

'Yes, I do remember. I had a dream, oh, such a nasty dream. I dreamed the pylon had . . . had come back again. It couldn't, Daddy, could it?'

'No, of course not.'

'Will you have a look, to make quite sure?'

'All right,' his father said. 'Anything for a quiet life.'

There followed a convulsion in the bedclothes, gusts of cool air rushed in. The room grew darker. Standing in front of the low casement window, Roger's tall figure blotted out the day-light. The outline of his arms down to his elbows, his shield-shaped back and straddled legs showed through the thin stuff of his pyjamas; his head, that looked small on his broad shoulders, seemed to overtop the window—but this was an optical illusion, as Laurie knew. Pulling the bedclothes round him he breathed hard, waiting for the verdict.

His father didn't speak at once. It'll do the boy good to get a bit worked up, he thought; strengthen the reaction when it comes. At length he said:

'Seems to be a lot going on over there.'

'A lot going on, Daddy?'

'Yes, men working, and so on.'

'What are they working at?'

'Can't you hear something?' his father asked, still without turning round.

Laurie strained his ears. Now he could hear it quite dis-tinctly borne in through the open window—the thudding and clanging of the workmen's hammers.

'What are they doing, Daddy?'

'Well, what do you think?'

Laurie's mind went blank. Often it happened that when his father asked him something, a shadow seemed to fall across his mind.

'Is it anything to do with the pylon?'

'You're getting warm now.'

'Are they—are they—?'

'Yes, they are. They're working on the concrete platform where the pylon used to stand.'

'They're not building it up again, are they, Daddy?'

'I couldn't tell you, old chap, but I wouldn't put it past them.'

Laurie's face fell. If only his father would turn round! His imploring glances made no impression on that broad straight back.

'But if they are, Daddy, I couldn't go on living here.'

'I'm afraid you'll have to, son, it's our home, you see. You'll get used to the new pylon, just as you got used to the old one.'

'I shan't, I shan't!' wailed Laurie, hungering more and more for the sight of his father's face. 'Can't you tell them not to do it, Daddy? Can't you *order* them?'

'I'm afraid not. They wouldn't pay any attention to me, Laurie.'

At the sound of his Christian name, which his father only used for grave occasions, and at the idea that there existed people for whom his father's word was not law, the bottom seemed to drop out of Laurie's world, and he began to whimper.

Then his father did turn round and looked down at his hapless offspring, from whom all stiffening of pride and self-control had melted, huddled in the bedclothes. He stifled his distaste and said what all along he had been meaning to say but had put off saying until the last of his son's defences should be down.

'Don't worry. I was only having you on. They're not building a new pylon. They're just breaking up the old one's concrete base. And high time, too. I can't think why they didn't do it before.'

As he turned away from the window the sunshine which his

body had displaced followed him back, filling the room with light. He sat down at the foot of the bed.

The effect of his long-delayed announcement had been magical: it surpassed his wildest hopes. Laurie was radiant, on top of his world, another creature from the abject object of a moment since. He tried to put his relief and gratitude into words, but could only smile and smile, in a defenceless almost idiotic way. To break the silence his father asked:

'What made you frightened of the pylon? Had it done you any harm?'

'Oh, yes,' said Laurie, recollection contracting his smile into a frown, 'it *had*.'

'What kind of harm?'

Laurie considered. How could he make the pylon's mischief plain to his father?

'Well, it made me sick for one thing.'

'Oh, that was just something you ate,' said Roger, well remembering it was not. 'We all eat things that disagree with us.'

'It wasn't only that. It . . . it *hurt* me.'

'How do you mean, hurt you?'

'In my dream it did.'

'In your dream? You'll have to tell me about your dream. But make it snappy—I've only got five minutes.'

'Yes . . . perhaps, sometime . . . You see, in my dream it was much stronger than I was, and I couldn't get to the top.'

'Why did you want to get to the top?'

'Well, I *had* to, because of the report, and to see what sort of report they would give me if I did get to the top.'

'I know what,' his father said. 'When you're a big chap, bigger than me, perhaps, you'd better be a pylon-builder. Do you know how much they earn?'

Pure numbers had an attraction for Laurie, though he wasn't good at maths.

'No, tell me.'

'Ten shillings an hour when they're on the ground, and a pound an hour when they're in the air ... You'd soon be a rich man, much richer than me. You'd like that, wouldn't you?'

'I don't want to be rich!' moaned Laurie. 'I want—' he stopped.

'Well, what do you want?'

'I want to be *safe*, and I shouldn't be if the pylon was there.'

'What nonsense!' said his father, at last losing patience. 'It's nothing to be afraid of.' He remembered his wife's words. 'It's only something men have made, and men can unmake. You could make one yourself with your Meccano—I'll show you how. It's only a few bits of metal—that's all it is.'

'But that's all the atom bomb is,' cried Laurie, 'just a few bits of metal, and everyone's afraid of it, even you are, Daddy!'

Roger felt the tables had been turned.

'You're right,' he said, 'I *am* afraid of it. But—' he tried to think of a way out—'I never *dream* about it.'

As always, his father's presence gave Laurie a feeling of helplessness; it was as if his thoughts could get no further than the figure turned towards him on the bed, whose pyjama-jacket, open to the morning airs, disclosed a hairy, muscular chest.

'But I can't help what I dream, can I?' he said.

His father agreed, and added, 'But you *can* help being frightened—frightened afterwards, I mean. You've only to think—'

'But I do think, Daddy. That's the worst of it.'

'I mean, think how absurd it is. If you were to dream about me—'

'Oh, but I have, ever so often.'

His father was taken aback, and tugged at his moustache.

'And were you frightened?'

It took Laurie some time to answer this. He sat up, wriggled his toes, on which his father's hand was resting, and said:

'Not *exactly* frightened.'

'Well,' said Roger, smiling, 'what effect, *exactly*, did I have on you?'

Laurie shook his head.

'I couldn't quite explain. Of course, in my dream you were different.'

'Nicer or nastier?'

'Well, not nastier—you couldn't be.'

Now it was Roger's turn to feel embarrassed. He stared at Laurie, and all at once Laurie's face turned scarlet.

'Oh, I didn't mean that, you *know* I didn't,' he pleaded. His hands traced circles on the rumpled bedclothes and his head oscillated with them. 'I said not nastier, because you never *are* nasty, so you couldn't be nastier, if you see what I mean.'

'I think I do,' his father said, mollified and more relieved than he was prepared to show, 'although I am nasty sometimes, I admit. But how was I different, in your dream?'

'That's just it, you weren't so nice.'

Roger didn't like the idea of being thought less nice, even in someone's dream. But he had to say something—he wouldn't let Laurie see he had been hurt.

'What was I like?' he asked, with assumed jauntiness.

'Oh, you were like yourself, to look at, I mean—not really like of course, because people never are, in dreams. But I always knew it was you.'

Less and less did Roger relish the idea of his dream personality being made known to him. Would it be cowardly to change the subject?

'Don't you ever dream about your mother?' he asked hopefully.

'Oh, no, *never*, nor about Susie or Victor. Only about you.'

There seemed to be no escape. Roger grasped the nettle.

'When you dream about me,' he asked, 'what do I *do*?'

'Oh, you don't *do* much, nothing to speak of. You're just *there*, you see.'

'I do see,' said Roger grimly, though he didn't really. 'And you don't like me being there?'

Laurie wriggled; his plump hands left off making circles on the sheet and clasped the front of his pyjama-jacket.

'No, I'm glad you're there, because I always feel safer when you are, but—'

'But what?' Let's get to the bottom of it now, thought Roger.

'Well, you make me think I've been doing something wrong.'

Roger's heart sank. It was too bad. Hadn't he always, throughout his parenthood, tried to give his children just the opposite impression—make them feel that what they did was *right*? Not so much with Victor and Susie, perhaps; he did tick them off sometimes, he really had to. But he had never succeeded in making them feel guilty; whereas with Laurie—

'Now listen,' he said. 'Stop fidgeting with your pyjamas or you'll be pulling off the buttons and then you *will* have done something wrong.' Switching himself round still farther on the bed he stretched his arms out towards Laurie and firmly imprisoned the boy's restless hands in his. 'Now listen,' he repeated, propelling Laurie gently to and fro, making the boy feel he was on a rocking-horse, 'dreams go by contraries, you know.'

'What does that mean, Daddy?'

'It means that when you dream something, you dream what is the opposite of the truth. Do you understand?'

'Yes, I think so.'

'So, if you dream about me and I seem nasty, or about the pylon and it seems nasty, it really means—' he stopped.

'Yes, go on, Daddy,' said Laurie, sleepily. He was enjoying the rocking motion—so different from the pylon's sickening lurches—and didn't want it to stop. 'Please go on,' he begged.

'It means that we're both—the pylon and me too, well, rather nice.'

Before Roger had time to see whether this thought was sinking in, there came a thunderous knocking at the door. Releasing Laurie's hands he pulled his pyjama-jacket round him and called out, 'Come in!'

There was a stampede into the room, a racket and a hubbub like a mob bursting in, and Susan and Victor, fully clothed, were standing by the bed.

'Oh, you *are* lazy,' Susan cried. 'You haven't even begun to dress, either of you, and you haven't heard the news.'

'What news?' Roger asked.

'Awful news, dreadful news, the worst. Isn't it, Victor?'

'It's simply frightful. It's the *end*,' Victor said. 'You'll never guess.'

Their faces beamed with happiness.

'Well, why are you so cheerful about it then?' their father asked.

'Oh, just because it is so horrible,' said Susan, and their faces glowed afresh. 'You'll never guess, and so we'll tell you.' She caught Victor's eye to give him his cue, and at the tops of their voices they chanted in unison:

'The pylon's coming back!'

Dead silence followed; even the impression of noise, which had been as strong as or stronger than the noise itself, was banished.

'You don't *say* anything,' said Susan, disappointed. 'We hoped you'd be . . . you'd be . . . just as upset as we are, and there you sit in your pyjamas . . . like . . . like . . .'

Her voice died away into the silence which had returned with double force, and seemed to occupy the room even more completely than the uproar had.

Roger's voice broke it.

'But you're wrong,' he said. 'They're not making a new pylon, they're only breaking up the platform of the old one.'

'No, no,' said Susie, dancing to and fro. 'It's you who are wrong, Daddy. You aren't *always* right, you know. You see we've been across and talked to the men themselves, and they say they are building a new pylon taller than the last—'

'A hundred and thirty-seven feet high,' put in Victor.

'Oh, yes, a huge great thing. We were so horrified we couldn't wait to tell you. It's true, Mummy, isn't it?"

She appealed to Anne who, hitherto unnoticed, was standing by the door.

'Yes, I'm afraid it is,' Anne said.

'There, we told you! And now the view will be spoilt again for ever!'

Stung in his masculine pride, shorn of his mantle of infallibility, Roger lost his temper. These wretched children! Ill-mannered brats, why had he spoilt them so? 'Now you clear out!' he thundered, adding, 'I don't mean you, Anne.' But his wife had already gone.

Laurie remained, but where? He had slipped down between the bedclothes, out of sight and almost out of mind. Now he came to the surface and let his stricken face be seen.

'Oh, Daddy!' he exclaimed. 'Oh, Daddy!' But what he meant by it he could not have told, so violent and discordant were the emotions that surged up in him. Indeed, they seemed to sound inside his head, drowning another noise that punctuated but did not break the silence: the hammerstrokes from which would rise a bigger and better pylon.

'I'm here, Laurie, I'm here!' his father said, but remembering the effect his presence had in Laurie's dreams he doubted whether it would be much consolation now; for was not Laurie always in a dream?